Endorsements

This is a delightful story of a curious little girl caught up in the tempest of World War II and carried by God's secret providence to discover his Son Jesus Christ.

- *Dr. Joel R. Beeke,*
President
Puritan Reformed Seminary

An excellent piece of writing! I enjoyed it very much! We all know that God is working out His great plan in His providence. Often, however, we fail to meditate on what seem to be the small events through which God is working. The book portrays the Great War going on in Europe and God's work in a small girl. What a God we have! What a story!"

- *Rev. Jerome Julien*
Minister of the Word, Emeritus

This dramatic and unusual war story about little Linnet and her family is also a biblical meditation on the passing of the old and the coming of the new. Farenhorst's compassion for her characters drew me into a world that I have been reliving and pondering as I see truth peeking out from unexpected places.

- Annie Kate Aarnoutse,
Tea Time with Annie Kate

This book is classic Christine. It is so easy to read – one gets quickly lost in the story – yet with rich, profound layering and depth. Truly a story for the whole family to laugh, cry, discuss, be challenged, and grow in grace. We simply loved this book.

- Mr. Maynard and Dr. Richelle Lanting

This is World War II through the eyes of a five-year-old Dutch girl who, we discover, knows absolutely nothing about God. For our own children, who may take always knowing God for granted, it will be eye-opening to follow what it's like, and how wonderful it is, for someone to be introduced to God for the first time. Linnet has the same wonderings any kid might have, but her wartime experiences also have her asking deeper questions, including a child's version of "God are you really there?"

This is that rarity that will appeal to all ages: the World War II setting and charming protagonist will grab your children; moms and dads will appreciate Linnet's questions and the opportunities they present to talk about God with our kids, and grandparents will get more than a little misty-eyed at just how beautifully this tale is told. I could not recommend it more highly!

- Jon Dykstra
Editor
Reformed Perspective

The New
Has Come

The New
Has Come

Christine Farenhorst

Brief summaries or quotations from this resource may be used with conventional acknowledgments in presentations, articles, and books, as well as digital comparatives. For all other uses, please write North Star Ministry Press LLC for permission.

Images: Keturah Tochijara

Author's Note: The town of Steendorp is a fictional town.

ISBN: 979-8-88526-107-4

Dedication

To Anco,
the father
of my children,
the grandfather
of my grandchildren
and a child
who is a new creation

Acknowledgment

To Norm Bomer,
for his contributions
to the final draft

He called a little child and had him stand among
them. And He said: "I tell you the truth, unless
you change and become like little children, you
will never enter the kingdom of heaven. There–
fore, whoever humbles himself like this child is
the greatest in the kingdom of heaven.
(Matthew 18:3–4)

On Faith

My little one, at mother's knee,
I write this for a chosen child
To dwell on godly history
Where Hebrew ancients domiciled.
To let you always be aware
That witness clouds without compare
Surround your paths – encircle ways –
Greatly enhancing all your days
With faith – the surety of hope –
The covenant's kaleidoscope.

A silver lining and the first
Resplendent rainbow for a song,
A silver lining and a thirst
To laugh at Noah's beastly throng.
Ah, Pentateuch – inspired cry
Singing a Sarah lullaby
Of Isaacs, Jacobs, and all such
That Laban men can never touch,
From Joseph and a dried-up well
To slavery of Israel.

Rameses building in a field
Of open sky and burning sun,
The warm and secret, reed–concealed,
Small basket of a child begun.
From plagues all ten and Red Sea moan,
To horse and rider overthrown,
Egyptians later could not see
The marvel of God's mystery
In taking for His very own
A Hebrew people, pilgrim prone.

It's in the wind and in the way
That Rahab's house did not fall down
And in the fields where foxes stray
Burned up the produce of a town.
It's in the Moabitic smiles
Of Ruth who walked Naomi's miles,
It's in the guarding sentinel

Who saved the friends of Daniel.
Remember how they overcame,
By faith, by faith, by faith, their fame.

What shall I add, my little one,
To such a faithful multitude?
When all is said and all is done,
They urge your own similitude.
From Gideon and David tones,
Who conquered kingdoms with God's stones,
To Hannah's prayers and Mary's song
Shouting for joy, exultant, strong.
By faith to these be reconciled,
Do not forget to be a child.

- Christine Farenhorst

Contents

Preface

As a child, I spent many summers on the island of Schiermonnikoog. Without fail, my father rented a cottage each year close to the dunes and, after an exciting trip on the ferry, we landed on the shore of this West Frisian municipality. Only sixteen kilometers long and four kilometers wide, it is presently the site of The Netherlands' first national park. The cottage we occupied, as most cottages on the island, lay within walking distance of the beach. Our family of eight, of which I was the youngest, loved this annual holiday! We collected shells, beheld jellyfish, crawled into abandoned bunkers, bicycled many paths, slept in dunes, and swam in the North Sea. For a change in venue, we also often hiked the woods. Here under the branches of coniferous trees, while reclining on a blanket or sitting with our backs against the trees, our father read amazing stories, while forest birds twittered away on boughs above our heads.

There were no computers, and I don't believe we had a telephone in the cottage either. There was an outside privy, and frequently spiders could be seen on the bedroom ceiling, causing my sisters much consternation. In the evening, before I was put to bed, my father would faithfully take me for a stroll to see the 'kippetjes', the chickens, housed in numerous coops that lined the lanes in and around town. Or he would locate a quiet spot in the dunes out of the wind's reach. Promising me that if I sat very still and did not sneeze or giggle, a rabbit or two or three would eventually emerge from their den to see us, I believed every word he said. It was a wonderful time of bonding and sharing, mostly, I think, because my father never failed to point out the wonders of creation.

The story of Linnet began as just that, a story on the island of Schiermonnikoog. As I kept on writing, it morphed into a novel perhaps because the immensity of God's choosing a child to be His very own is beyond thought and understanding. May this narrative move readers to marvel at the splendor of God's election, and search out the freedom that is theirs in Christ. And may they remember the importance of believing in the God of creation. For God Who said: *"Let light shine out of darkness, made His light shine in our hearts to give us the light of the knowledge of God's glory displayed in the face of Christ."* (2 Cor. 4:6)

Therefore, if anyone is in Christ, he is a new creation. The old has passed away; behold, the new has come. (2 Cor. 5:17)

1

A person advancing in age is often perceived to be more un-hurried in movement and deliberation than was his wont when younger. It is also said that a dog slows down when getting on in years. Left hind leg leisurely following his left foreleg, the animal steps towards a perceived goal in a ponderous way. Even a clock or a watch, whose mechanism stems from yesteryear, can run seconds, minutes, or even hours behind time. A seed, however, planted and destined by God for eternity always sprouts and sends forth its shoots at the correct pace and at the right time; there is no age differential, no gender or race distinction, and no status symbol that could prevent that new creation from germinating at its ap-pointed time.

****

Freddy was an ornithologist. In other words, he investigated and studied birds. Frequently regaling me with stories of gulls, os-preys, nightingales, and woodpeckers, he insisted that since

childhood he had been fascinated by the habits and lifestyles of creatures with wings. Endowed with a great amount of patience, he rather felt that he met the qualifications for birdwatching exceedingly
well. He defined those qualifications as possessing an ability to wait
calmly without complaining; as owning a steady temperament; as
having an ability to relax; and as holding an enormous love for
"aves" (which he told me meant "birds" in Latin).

Freddy was a member of the Wilson Society of Birds, a society
formed in 1886, and he regularly read the Wilson Bulletin to me before I fell asleep at night. Pearls of wisdom about his feathered
friends were second nature to him. It's not only fine feathers that
make fine birds, he would say, as he pointed out a nearby strutting
crow. Or he would apprise me of the fact that birds had never lied
to him and had given him their best songs from the time they woke
up until they went to bed. Aware that he wrote a great many things
down in a lined notebook each day, a very impressive notebook, I
was convinced that he was brilliant. Freddy wore glasses, had blue
eyes, a big smile, and blond, curly hair. He stood about six feet tall
and I followed him around like a puppy dog.

Thea was an artist – the kind who drew pictures. She loved
birds and other animals with the same intensity that Freddy loved
them. Setting up her easel and mixing her colors, capturing and
watching wildlife on both canvas and paper, was her passion. Unlike Freddy, who was tall and blond, Thea was dark–haired like a
gypsy, measuring only about five foot three. Sloe–eyed, with high
cheekbones and olive skin, she was very beautiful, effortlessly moving with a grace that I was sure only fairy queens possessed. Besides
sketching her beloved animals, Freddy and I formed Thea's existence. It gave me great joy to be part of her delight, for I instinctively

felt that everyone needs to belong and that everyone needs to be loved. I had lived with Freddy and Thea ever since I could remember, and I called them by their first names. This did not seem strange to me at all, as it had been my custom since I could first speak.

Freddy, Thea, and I lived on Schiermonnikoog, a part of the Frisian Island group (or Wadden Sea Islands) which forms an archipelago extending five hundred kilometers along Dutch, German, and Danish coastlines. The Wadden Sea is a shallow body of water in which the islands lie, and it stretches all the way from Den Helder in the northwest of Holland, to the peninsula of Skallingen in Denmark. Consisting of sand flats, the sea is a saltwater tidal delta intersected by deep channels and connected to the North Sea through inlets. The Dutch islands of the archipelago are named Texel, Vlieland, Terschelling, Ameland, and Schiermonnikoog. Schiermonnikoog, the smallest inhabited island of the group, lies the farthest east. Sixteen kilometers long and four kilometers wide, ebb and tide, sky and water, birds, rabbits, cows, and dunes abound. It was truly a wonderful place to live, and it was the cradle which rocked me into childhood.

There was only one village on the island and it bore the same name as the island – Schiermonnikoog. The native population consisted of approximately six hundred souls, but we, Thea, Freddy, and myself, lived outside the village. Although we were not hermits, we were content to live a somewhat solitary existence. Beside tidal flats and wetlands, we inhabited a small cottage past the dunes on the eastern side of the island. It was rented out to us by a local farmer. A minute cottage, the main floor living area measured only some four and a half meters by four and a half meters. Upstairs there were two rooms, although perhaps the small recess in the hallway which held my bed could not properly be called a room. But after

Thea hung a curtain around my small nook, it became a truly wonderful, miniature chamber. There was a window above my cot, and if I stood on top of the cot, leaning on the windowsill, I could see the smooth slip face of a dune belt not too far away. Freddy's and Thea's room was larger than my bed area and held an oak bed – a truly magnificent piece of furniture. Our cat, named Belle because she wore one, (Thea said it was only fair to the birds), often curled up on the four–poster. There was a pump a few feet from the backdoor, an outhouse to the left of it, and a small vegetable garden, encased with chicken wire because of the rabbits, just inside our back picket fence. The dunes were close and the sound of both seagulls and the sea washed over us night and day. Beyond the dunes lay the Wadden Sea. The Wadden Sea was connected to the North Sea, and the North Sea was a shallow arm of the Atlantic Ocean. Where the ocean went I did not know.

It was on a Thursday morning that I met Marieke for the first time. I remember the day well because it was one of the days on which I was often sent into town to fetch supplies – those supplies being sugar, tea, and biscuits the day that I met Marieke. Returning from the village as I walked along the sandy path towards our cottage, I heard the sound of sobbing coming from behind one of the dunes. I was all of five years old and walked tall and proud, swinging the green cloth bag Thea had given me to carry the food.

"Now mind you, Linnet," she had said to me before I left, "don't dawdle and don't lose the bag."

"I wouldn't lose the bag," I replied indignantly.

Thea smiled and said, "Remember the *koek* (cake) which you fed to the seagulls last month?"

"Well," I replied, "that was different – that was because one of the seagulls had a broken wing and could not forage for itself."

"Yes," she replied, "so I'm only reminding you to keep things in the bag."

I raised my eyebrows in a hurt, insulted sort of way, and she hid a grin behind her hand, which made me all the more offended as I marched off. Coming back from the village, I took the long way home, following a path which snaked through the dunes and which allowed me to gaze my fill at the white breakers crashing onto the shore. It was a windy and glorious day, and I loved seeing the pull of the roaring surf on the wet sand. And yet through all that noise I distinctly heard something that didn't belong – something that didn't mix with the waves embracing the shoreline. It was the sound of sobbing, of pitiful sobbing. Birds don't sob and certainly the rabbits who frequented the dunes didn't cry (they only screamed if they were frightened). And then I saw her. That is to say, I saw what seemed to be a red jacket crowned with red hair. A small girl inhabited the jacket and she was curled up into a ball under the overhang of a dune. I dropped the bag and made my way over.

"Are you hurt?" I inquired politely, that being the most common reason of tears in my own case.

The sobbing abruptly stopped. Slowly the jacket and the red hair sat up. Dark blue eyes met mine. They were the sort of color of which violets were made and reminded me of meadow thistle, a purplish weed that grew here and there in abundance.

"Why are you crying?" I went on considerately, minding the little niceties that Thea had taught me to use with strangers, "Did you fall down? Or," I went on curiously, "are you maybe lost?"

Two plump hands rubbed the wet eyes and the girl, mute except for some recurring sniffles, stared. Eventually wiping her nose on the back of her jacket, she continued to consider me for some time before standing up.

"What's your name?" I probed on.

"Marieke Blom."

The answer was whisper–spoken. It was so soft it was almost carried off in the wind and the waves.

"Mine is Linnet."

Marieke was about my height and she straightened her shoulders as she stood. Putting her hands behind her back, she pursued her appraisal of me.

"Why were you crying?" I repeated the question only to get her to talk. But at those words her face crumpled back into woe and her chin quivered.

"You can tell me," I offered, feeling like Thea who was my comfort in fear and distress, "and maybe I can help you."

"Well," she began, as she sat back down in the sand, "I asked *Mem* where I came from and she told me . . . ." Her chin wobbled badly at this point and I walked over and sat down in the dunes next to her.

"What did your *Mem* say?"

"She said," Marieke went on, "she said that she found me under . . . under a cabbage leaf."

I stared at her. Her red hair and her violet eyes did not belie the fact that it seemed possible that she had indeed been found under a cabbage.

"Was it a red cabbage?" I wondered out loud.

Marieke did not answer, but her body, next to mine, began to shiver once more with crying.

"Well," I suggested practically, "to be found under a red cabbage is good. It gave you wonderful purple eyes and it seems to me that being found under a red cabbage is better than being found under an onion. Imagine that! You would forever be crying, and who would want to be close to you if you had been found under an onion, because you would smell."

Marieke stared at me for a moment and then smiled, smiled even as a tear coursed down her cheek. Encouraged, I went on.

"Or imagine that you had been found in the dune grass, then your *Mem* might not have found you at all, there is so much of it. And," I went on, inspired by the fascinated look on Marieke's face, "you might have had green spikes for fingers."

Marieke's smile changed into a giggle. "Where did your *Mem* tell you that you were found?" she then demanded.

Having never thought about it before, I considered the question seriously. Perhaps Freddy and Thea had found me under the Marram grass – grass that grew in all the dunes close to our little cottage. Its fibrous matted roots bound the sand down, Thea had once told me, and helped other plants to grow. Or perhaps I had come out of one of the eggs that Freddy often found as he birded. After all, my name was Linnet. But I truly did not really know. I turned to face Marieke, whose violet eyes were eagerly fixed on my face. Perhaps she wanted me to say that I had also been found under a cabbage leaf, and I was tempted to lie just to make us friends.

"I don't know," I eventually answered, "but I belong to Freddy and Thea."

"Are they your *Mem* and *Heit*?"

"I live with them."

"Then they must be your *Mem* and *Heit*."

Marieke sighed a deep sigh as she spoke, rocking her body back and forth before she smiled at me again and I smiled back.

"It's all right then," she said, as she got up, "to be found under a red cabbage. I didn't know whether it was all right you see, and I was afraid that one day I might be eaten."

I got up too. "I wouldn't worry if I were you," I fibbed. "Parents of red cabbage children never eat them. I read it in a book."

"You can read?"

Marieke was impressed.

"Yes, Thea taught me to read. And Freddy helped with lessons when he was not busy reading his own books. I can read the names of many birds. I do love birds, don't you?"

Marieke looked doubtful. "Well, some of them," she slowly acknowledged, "but I'm afraid when I hear the owl screech."

"Oh," I interjected, eager to tell her that she need not be scared, that the owl was really very nice, when we heard Marieke's name being called – called loudly and imperiously.

"That's *mem*," Marieke said, "and I better go, because I did run away from her and she'll be very angry if I don't come back soon."

Then she was gone, up the dune side and over it. She was gone before I could tell her that barn owls, for example, are super soft and that I always feel sorry for them when it rains because their feathers are not waterproof and they get soaking wet. I wanted to tell her that when Freddy told me this, I had asked him if we could make little umbrellas for barn owls and that he had laughed and laughed.

Later, at home, when Thea asked me where the green grocery bag was, my mind flew back to the space in the dunes where I had dropped it. She raised her eyebrows and then I had to return and fetch it so that we could have biscuits with our tea that afternoon. It was only when Thea came to tuck me into my cot that evening that I finally asked her the question which had been nagging at me ever since I had spoken with Marieke.

"Thea, where do I come from?"

Thea had been about to kiss me goodnight and mind me to go to sleep right away, but at the query she sank to her haunches in a surprised manner.

"What makes you ask me that, Linnet?"

So I told her about my conversation with Marieke. She was quiet for a very long time afterwards and stroked hair away from my forehead.

"You know, don't you," she began, "that Freddy and I lived on the mainland for awhile."

I nodded. Indeed, I did know that. They sometimes spoke of it. Freddy had been the groundskeeper on an estate. He had met Thea at a conference on wildlife conservation sometime during the 1920s. They had liked each other very much and here they were together.

"We were not," Thea continued, speaking somewhat hesitantly, "able to have children," and at this point she began to stroke my hair rather fiercely, causing me to cry out in pain.

"I'm sorry, Sweet Thing," she said, kissing my forehead and sighing before she continued. "I was very sad and so was Freddy, about the not having children, you see. And then one day, a day when I was feeling especially sad, an evening actually, I went for a walk."

"Was it a dark walk?" I asked, mindful of the fact that Freddy and Thea never allowed me to walk out at night.

"Well, it was windy, but the moon was out," Thea answered, "and I had a lantern, you see."

"Oh." I moved my head from side to side and studied Thea's face, surprised to see tears coursing down her cheeks. "Why are you crying, Thea?"

"Because," she answered, "the memory of this is very dear and special to me, Linnet. You see, I found you on this walk."

"You found me? Under a cabbage leaf?"

"Yes, I did find you, and no, not under a cabbage leaf. As I said, I was feeling sad. Freddy and I had been together for more than twelve years, and we still had no children. I did not suppose that I would ever hold a baby in my arms. Well, on this walk, even though the moon was shining, there were dark periods when the clouds covered the moon. I was moving the lantern from left to right to see my way clear on the sand path on which I was walking, and suddenly I heard this tiny sound traveling through the dark. It was a hushed sound and I heard it through the wind. It came from the right side of the lane on which I was walking. There was a field on either side, you see. I thought at first it was an animal. But the sound, although almost inaudible, kept on, and it sounded so pitiful and wretched, that I moved towards it. There was a ditch full of duckweed between myself and the field to my right. The ditch was not wide, so I jumped it. Still, even though I shone the lantern carefully, I could not perceive what was making the haunting, plangent sound. That is, not until I noted a hole, a rather large hole, a hole looking almost like a pocket–sized grave."

She stopped and I fondled her hand.

"What then, Thea? What was in the hole?"

"There was a little box in the hole, Linnet. A tiny, wooden box, a little coffin almost. The wood was white pine and the sound came from inside the box. It was a weak cry, a whimper, a whine almost.

I knelt down on the soil, put the lantern next to me and lifted that little coffin out of the hole. Its lid had not been nailed down. Whoever had put the box into the hole had not done that. My arms trembled when I lifted the lid."

Thea stopped and I pulled her arm.

"Then what happened, Thea? What did you see? Was I in the box?"

Thea looked at me and nodded, even as her eyes filled with tears. Downstairs I could hear Freddy messing about with the tea that he and Thea would drink after she had tucked me in. Perhaps they would also listen to the radio. I often heard them listen to the radio at night.

"Well, I opened the box very carefully," Thea's voice was quivery now, "and I think that I have never seen anything as beautiful as you were, my little Linnet, as you lay there in that little box. You wore a bonnet, a blue bonnet embroidered with stars, and you were wrapped in a white blanket."

"Were my eyes open?"

I didn't know why I asked that. But I wanted to be able to see Thea in my mind, even as she had seen me at that moment.

"Did you lift me out of the box?" I went on, eager to know exactly what had happened, "and did you cuddle me straight away?"

"I was afraid to lift you out," Thea said, beginning to stroke my hair again, "I was afraid the whole thing was a dream and that I would wake up. Sometimes," she went on, now putting her hands into her lap, "I still think it's all a dream and that you won't be there in the morning."

"But I am," I said rather forcefully, sitting up in the bed and turning onto my knees, even as I took hold of Thea's hands, "and I am your girl always and always, as you tell me every day."

"Yes," Thea smiled through her tears, "and you were not dead and you did open your eyes and you did stop your whimpering as soon as you saw me."

"Did I?"

I was quiet for a moment then, quiet with the wonder of the whole story. And then the questions spurted out again.

"Did you lift me up then? Did you carry me back to Freddy? And could you jump over the ditch while you were carrying me and the box and the lantern?"

"I did lift you up. But it was so windy that I put you back into the box to keep you from the chill. Then I jumped over the ditch with you in the box and I put you down on the path before going back for the lantern," she replied. "And then I carefully walked home, cradling the box with you in it."

"What did Freddy say when you came home? Was he surprised?"

Thea now grinned and I was glad of the grin. There was such a sadness in me when she cried. Sometimes, when she thought I didn't notice, Thea would weep in her bedroom. And Freddy would go and sit with her and I knew it had something to do with what had happened to her a long time ago.

"Freddy was very surprised indeed!"

"Did he take off his glasses? Was he that surprised?"

"Yes, he did take off his glasses. And then . . . ."

"What then?"

"Well, then we sat together on the old couch – the couch we have now that we took with us from the mainland. And we looked at you for five, ten minutes, maybe even half an hour. You were very content and stared back at us with your light brown eyes, eyes the color of a linnet. That's what Freddy immediately thought of at any rate. Then he quoted a poem by Tennyson."

She stopped and smiled to herself.

"What was the poem, Thea?"

"Well, some of it goes like this, little Linnet. And Thea recited:

"I envy not in any moods
The captive void of noble rage,
The linnet born within the cage,
That never knew the summer woods;"

Thea stopped with a faraway look on her face.

"That sounds beautiful," I said, "but I wasn't in a cage, Thea. You just told me that I was in a box."

Thea smiled and whispered, "Yes, you were."

"Were there more words to the poem, Thea?"

"Well, yes," she said, "and these were the last words."

"I hold it true, whate'er befall;
I feel it, when I sorrow most;
'Tis better to have loved and lost
than never to have loved at all."

I was quiet and then repeated, "Than never to have loved at all. But you love me, don't you, Thea?"

"I surely do," she answered.

"And you will never lose me, will you, Thea?"

"Never, Little Thing."

"What did you do next, after the poem, I mean?"

"Freddy got up. He kissed you and he kissed me and went to visit the farmer down the road, asking if he could have some goat milk. He asked for a bottle as well. You were quiet the whole time he was gone. I had been afraid that you might cry. You were such a tiny thing, but you seemed very happy with our company. It appeared to me that we were all that you had needed to make you stop whimpering."

"Did you talk to me, Thea, when Freddy was gone? And what did you say?"

"I sang to you, Little Thing. I sang all the lullabies that I knew and that I had never been able to sing until you came."

I sighed. It was a good story and it filled my whole head and heart. Thea began to sing very softly.

> *"A sorrowful, small girl sat down,*
> *Right by the river side,*
> *She sobbed and tears fell on her gown,*
> *Her parents dear had died."*

It was a sad song, and few were the times that I had heard Thea sing it. I liked her other lullabies better.

"Had they died, Thea?"

"We never could find out, Little Thing," Thea answered, looking down at the floor now. " Freddy tried and tried, but there was no trace of anyone or anything. We petitioned for adoption and . . . .

"What does that mean?"

"It means that we asked the Civil Court if you could become a real member, a true part of our family; it means that the two of us,

Freddy and I, became three; and it means that the three of us are now one together."

"What if," I posited, "my real parents had come back, Thea? What if that had happened? Or did you suppose that I didn't have any?"

Thea did not answer, but abruptly got up and left my little bedroom. I could hear her go downstairs and I supposed that I was to go to sleep. Snuggling back under the covers, I gazed up at the window above my cot. Outside were the dunes and the great North Sea and here I was in my snug and cozy room, part of Freddy and Thea, because they had found me in a little box. I was a present. Too bad that there had not been a ribbon on the box. I yawned. Footsteps came up the stairs. A moment later, Freddy sat down on the edge of the cot and his arms enfolded me.

"So, Little Linnet, you have heard the story of the box?"

I nodded and then giggled. "You were surprised, Freddy, weren't you, when I came out of the box. Thea says you even took off your glasses."

"I love you, Little Thing, and only came up to tell you that. And now you're teasing me because I took off my glasses?"

In mock humor, he made as if to leave immediately, but I held him fast. And he hugged me so hard that my ribs hurt – but it was a good hurt.

2

Freddy often gave me history lessons as we walked together. He told me that the island we lived on, Schiermonnikoog, had probably first been inhabited by monks, Cistercian monks, way back in the thirteen hundreds. The word "Schiermonnikoog," he explained, was really three words: *Schier*, meaning "grey," *monnik*, meaning "monk," and *oog*, carrying the double meaning of "eye" and "island."

"Who owns the island, Freddy?"

We were sitting on the edge of a farmer's field. Freddy had recorded a northern lapwing in that very place the day before and was hoping for a second sighting. Though not uncommon, Freddy wanted to be able to write down in his notebook that plovers returned to certain areas if they liked the vegetation.

"What is the lapwing's species, Little Thing?" Freddy inquired, ignoring my island ownership question totally.

"Vanellus, Vanellus," I answered promptly, having been schooled by him in species since I was big enough to speak.

"And why is it called lapwing?"

"Because it has a slow wingbeat."

Freddy clucked approvingly.

"All right, Little Genius, now I will answer your question about who owns the island. Until recently, the island was owned by the German Count Hartwig Arthur Berthold Graf von Bernstorff. I saw the Count once. His rather long, long name struck me as rather funny because he was a short, short man, a man who was balding, a man who had a big, black mustache, and a man who wore an expensive coat. But he died a little while ago and now his son, Berthold von Bernstorff, owns the island. The von Bernstorff family bought the island from Mr. Banck back in the 1800s, way before your time."

It was quiet for a bit. A bird flew by, but it was not a lapwing. Freddy did not pay it any attention, but went on talking.

"Now Mr. Banck was, among other things, a poet and a pleasant man. He planted a pine tree forest on the island to encourage trade in wood. As well, he built the first harbor and began a nautical college."

"What is nautical?"

"Nautical means having to do with the sea. A nautical college is a school where students learn about all manner of things that have to do with the sea or the ocean."

Freddy stopped, took off his glasses, wiped them, and put them back on before he continued.

"And what else have I told you about Mr. Banck, Linnet?"

I reflected, remembered, and recited.

"Mr. Banck was a rich lawyer from The Hague. He paid for the building of the Banckpolder and its dike to protect the island and the village from the sea. The polder was enclosed by the dike to keep the seawater out. It made the farmers very happy, because it gave them more land to grow crops. Mr. Banck loved watching the sea, and there is a bench on the sea wall made out of stone. It is called Banck's Bench."

"Very good, Linnet," Freddy praised me, "and now put this in your memory hat as well. The marshlands behind the dike did became very fertile, but they also caused some problems between the farmers who had polder land and the farmers who farmed close to the village. Those farmers close to the village could see that the land by the polder was much better than their own, and it made them a little jealous. But still, everyone pretty well liked Mr. Banck, so no real problems occurred."

"Also, Freddy," I added, "Mr. Banck built a hotel where people could come and stay in the summer. And he planted sand reed . . . ."

Here Freddy stopped me.

"And what is another name for sand reed, Miss Encyclopedia?"

"Marram grass," I answered promptly, for did not Thea bring it home occasionally and together we wove the grass into little mats which we used here and there in corners of the cottage or placed them on the table for decoration?

Freddy rubbed his hands together, something he always did when he was pleased. "You're a good student, Linnet, with a phenomenal photographic memory, and I'm proud of you."

We had gotten up and were beginning our trek home. "Freddy, do you think that I will ever see the Count's son? And if I did, do you think that he would build me a bench?" I asked the question as we were walking back to the cottage.

"I don't think so, Little Thing. And who wants to see a Count anyway? I would rather see a merlin."

"*Falco columbarius*," I spouted automatically and Freddy clapped me on the shoulder.

"Excellent, Little Thing, you surpass my greatest expectations."

I grinned.

All this time we had not sighted even one lapwing. But it was always enjoyable to be out together. The island was a wonderful place for birds and for people. I conjectured that, in spite of what Freddy had said, perhaps the Count might be into birdwatching, and that we might see him in an expensive coat walking the seashore or lazing in a dune pan. At that point, I would walk up to him and say, *Hello, Count. My name is Linnet.*"

Freddy pushed my back.

"Come on, Linnet, walk a little faster. Thea probably has some hot tea and magnificent cake waiting for us."

I nodded absently, at the same time pulling leaves off the branches of a nearby bush. Many berry– bearing bushes and trees were native to the island. There were hawthorns, buckthorns, elderberries, blackberries and wild roses. Freddy was not fond of the hawthorn. I had once stepped onto one of its thorns when I was two and a half, and it had embedded deeply into my foot. He'd had to take it out with tweezers and I had squealed louder than a screech owl in the night.

"I thought the island was Dutch, Freddy," I contemplated out loud as we walked on, stroking the leaves in my hand. "If a German Count owns it, doesn't that make the island German?"

Freddy didn't answer, and looking up, I could see that he was scowling.

"What's the matter, Freddy?"

"Well, Little Thing, it's not easy to explain. But I have a feeling that we're in for some very bad weather."

"But there's not even one cloud in the sky, Freddy."

Scanning the horizon, I could only make out the *Vuurtoren*, the Fire Tower, in the distance. King William III of Holland had requested that the island build this northern lighthouse as well as its sister tower, the white southern lighthouse. Both were finished in 1854. I liked the northern lighthouse best, because of its fiery color and because of its rotating light. That was, Freddy had explained, so that it could guide ships through the North Sea. The red tower was 37 meters high and you had to climb 153 steps to get to the top. I knew this to be a fact, because Freddy and Thea had taken me to its very summit. I had counted the steps up, every single one of them and had been thoroughly convinced that once I reached the very top of the tower I would be able to touch the clouds with my fingers. I was heavily disappointed. Things were not always what they seemed to be. I was not able do it.

"So what do you mean, bad weather, Freddy?" I persisted.

He sighed and sat down on a dune.

"Well, perhaps it is time for us to have a talk, Little Thing. You know that Thea and I listen to the radio, don't you?"

I nodded. Sometimes they let me listen too, and I would hear jolly music or choirs singing. And on occasion Thea and I danced together.

"Well," Freddy went on, "we often hear news on the radio about other places. We hear what is happening in other countries."

I stared at him. News, other countries? What did all that have to do with bad weather?

"Every so often, when people talk about bad weather, Linnet, they refer to what is happening around them. Bad weather might mean that bad times are coming . . . times of trouble . . . or times of difficulty."

He stopped and, totally baffled, I sat down next to him. "I don't understand. What do you mean, Freddy?"

"It's hard to explain, Linnet. You've lived here on the island most of your life, if not all of it, really. And it is easy and agreeable to live here. But there are other places, places where people don't have a cozy cottage like we do. Some of these people have problems – money problems, no work, and no food, and sometimes these people have to leave where they live so they won't get hurt."

I had absolutely no idea what or whom he was talking about, but I felt compassion stir up within me for these unknown persons.

"Who are these people that have to leave? And why would they get hurt?"

Freddy was silent now. I pondered his words. It was true. It was not hard to live where we lived. I went to bed promptly at seven each night, unless Freddy was taking me to see rabbits by moonlight, which he sometimes did. And we had food. There were lovely breakfasts and lunches and suppers. Thea made good meals. And then before bed there were the stories – stories which both Freddy and Thea told. There were fairy tales, and funny tales, and . . . Freddy began again, began right through the middle of my thoughts.

"There is a German man – not a big man to look at really – but he is not a good man, Little Thing."

"A little man like the Count?" I interrupted.

Freddy didn't comment, but went on.

"This man, Linnet, wants to do bad things to a great many people. He wants to take their homes away and, he also wants to . . . to kill them."

Freddy stopped again and pulled at some dune grass. He seemed to be lost in thought. I pondered the fact that we lived in a small cottage. But it was big and cozy for the three of us. I loved the way it stood behind the dunes and the way its walls were white and the roof was green. It was my home, but what if a little man came to take it away? How could a little man take away our cottage anyway? No one, no matter how big, could carry a cottage. And why might anyone want to kill us? I was about to ask Freddy these things when he continued – continued in a rather monotone, tired voice.

"This man, Linnet, has a hunger to eat people. He has a great thirst to swallow up countries and make himself fat by doing so. He is not a good man and I'm afraid that there's going to be a war."

"What is war, Freddy?"

Some seagulls flew overhead, mewing as they went, capturing my attention at once. I rather liked the sound they made. Freddy said that seagulls hid when they were ready to die and that is why we did not often find a dead seagull. A baby seagull was called a chick and . . . again Freddy interrupted my wandering thoughts.

"War is not nice, Little Thing. It is when people fight one another, often killing each other in the process. A number of months ago, the German man's army invaded the country of Poland. Two days later, England and France, other countries which were friends with Poland, declared war on Germany. That's a lot of countries fighting."

I did not comprehend everything he was saying, but the word fighting was familiar.

"Will the fighting come here, Freddy?"

"Holland is our country, Linnet, and it is neutral. That means we don't want to fight. Maybe we should fight to help the other countries, because Germany is hurting them. And perhaps if we do join the fight, there might come a time when we might have to hide."

"Where would we hide, Freddy? Would we hide in the dunes? Or perhaps go into town?"

Freddy shrugged.

"Well," I went on, eager to offer suggestions, longing to be helpful, for I did not like the drained, weary look that had settled on Freddy's face. "Perhaps we could go to Banck's Polder and ask some farmer to hide us in a barn?"

Freddy now laughed, and I was relieved.

"Don't you worry your little brown-haired head about it, Linnet. Thea and I will figure something out."

I did have brown hair. It was not black like Thea's was, but like hers it did hang past my shoulders. I loved dancing while it bounced off my back. Thea often tied it in a pony tail, and I would pretend I was a pony, whinnying and neighing as I had seen horses in island fields do. I shook it now as I continued to probe Freddy.

"But will you tell me after you figure it out? And will it be soon that we have to hide?"

"I don't know, Linnet. We listen to the radio every day and every evening for information that might help us make sense of these things. There are already some Germans living on the island . . . I'm not sure . . . ."

"What about Belle, Freddy?" I interrupted, a thought suddenly striking me. "How can Belle hide?"

Freddy grimaced, whether in anger or exasperation I don't know. "I think Belle will be fine, Linnet. Don't forget that she sometimes disappears for days and days and then we can't find her."

This was true, and I sighed in relief. "Will it only be for a few days then, that we have to hide?"

There was no immediate answer. In the distance, sunbathing on sandbanks, I could spot two gray seals.

"Will the seals have to hide too, Freddy? Does this man eat seals too?"

"I don't know, Linnet. I just know that he has a lot more tanks, airplanes, and soldiers than Holland has."

Freddy sounded a bit cross now, and I knew enough not to ask any more questions. So I watched the seals. A mother seal cares for her young only about four weeks. And if something dangerous happens, she looks out for herself, not her pups. I was surely glad that Freddy and Thea were thinking about looking after me if there was to be a war with fighting. Once, when I was swimming with Thea near the shore, paddling was actually more like it because we were in water that was quite shallow, a seal had moved close to us. Moving his hind flippers from side to side, he was using his front flippers to steer towards us. I clung to Thea, for the seal was large. He was only curious, Thea had said soothingly, putting her arms around me, curious about who we were and what we were doing. Well, if there were a war, then surely the seals could dive down deep and deeper into the North Sea and no one would be able to harm them.

"It's time to go, Linnet." Freddy suddenly stood up, stretching his arms out high above his head. "I don't want you to be scared, Little Thing," he said after he finished his stretch, "but it's best to know when something unusual or perhaps frightening might happen. That way you can prepare yourself, and that way it's not as scary."

I nodded, feeling quite like a grownup as I reached for Freddy's hand. He took it, squeezed it and winked at me, and I winked back. I loved Freddy so much! And later, back in the cottage, Thea did have hot tea waiting, and she had baked a yellow cake. It was a wonderful treat, and we praised it so much she let us have a second slice.

3

Freddy and Thea let me listen to the radio one evening in May. It was May the 9th, actually, and the eve of Thea's birthday. I was very excited to be allowed to stay up and listen with them.

"The Prime Minister of Holland will speak to the country at 9:30 tonight, Linnet," Freddy solemnly declared at supper time, "and as this is an historic occasion, we will waive your bedtime."

"Waive?"

"We will give it up; we will not insist on your regular bedtime," he explained.

"Oh."

I curled up on the couch and tried to make out Thea's red geraniums blooming in the window boxes hanging just outside the cottage window. I had watered them for her that day. I loved geraniums, their abundance of blooms, and their strong smell. But it was dark out now, and I could barely make them out through the thin curtains. I snoozed my way through the evening, wondering if a prime minister and a count were alike. Would the count's son listen to the broadcast too? The rounded wooden radio box suddenly crackled, and Freddy and Thea, who had been catnapping as well, automatically sat up. Our clock had just chimed the half hour. It was 9:30 already, and I had been leaning comfortably into Thea's side. When she sat up straight, I almost fell over. A mild voice began speaking.

"That's the Prime Minister, Mr. De Geer," Freddy whispered by way of explanation.

The truth was that Mr. De Geer sounded no different from any other man I had ever heard speak. Perhaps I had expected, because he was, after all, supposed to be a very important man, a loud, commanding voice. But his tone had little inflection and carried no authority.

"There is nothing to worry about," he informed us as we sat next to one another on the couch in the cottage, "nothing at all. There will be no war. It will not happen. I have spoken with influential government officials . . . ."

At this point, Freddy and Thea looked at each other. I knew the look. It was one they exchanged when they were not sure about something, a look that was both distrustful and rather incredulous.

"I think the man is . . . ." Thea shoved her elbow into Freddy's side. "He is the Prime Minister, Freddy."

"Yes, but he is both misinformed and uninformed."

"He says there won't be any war, Freddy," I trumpeted out, yawning at the same time.

Thea took me to bed. "Sleep well, Little Thing."

"Good night, Thea."

I had seen Marieke only once after that first meeting in the dunes. We had waved to one another in the village street a few times, grinning broadly as we passed. She would be holding her mother's hand, and I would be holding my grocery bag. But we had not really conversed or gotten to know one another better. Very early that morning of May 10, 1940, the morning after Mr. De Geer's broadcast, I did see her again. Freddy had sent me into town to pick up some *boterkoek*, buttercake – a cake which he had ordered before-hand without Thea knowing about it. Before the regular store hours, I snuck out of the house, wanting to make sure Thea did not see me. I bumped into Marieke just after sunup on the main village road on my way to the baker's shop.

"Hello, Marieke."

She was wearing her red coat and didn't see me, as she was studying the ground rather intently. Startled, she looked up, and upon seeing me, smiled instantly. "Hello, Linnet."

"How are you?" I went on, eager for conversation, "I'm going to the baker's to pick up a cake for Thea's birthday."

"A cake?"

Her smile grew bigger and the copper–colored hair tucked into her red collar glowed. It was, I reflected as I looked at her, like the sun rising in the morning. But then, just as quickly as Marieke's face had blossomed into a smile, it slumped into sadness. In just the frac-tion of a moment, her freckles grew dull and her nose became pinched as if she were going to cry.

"What's the matter?" I said, remembering the dune conversa-tion, contemplating whether crying was her second nature and won-dering if perhaps her *Mem* had told her something else pertaining to where she came from.

"I . . ." she feebly began, her mouth twisting in a funny way, "I . . . my *Heit* and *Mem* say we're going away, away from the island. It's war now, you know, . . . and . . . .

I repeated rather vehemently, "Who told you it's war? War is when people fight and kill each other. Besides that," I added importantly, "we listened to the radio last night and I heard the Prime Minister say that there won't be any war."

Pointing to the almost vacant street, I went on. "There's no one outside killing anyone, is there?"

She shook her head, simultaneously rubbing her eyes. Her square, front teeth showed up in a cautious grin.

"Well, then," I sensibly went on, "it can't be war, can it? In a war people fight and kill each other. Why don't you come to the bakery with me and we'll pick up the cake. It always smells so good in there that you never feel sad standing by the counter."

I took her by the hand and we amiably strolled to the bakery together. When we got to the little shop, however, and tried to get in, the door was locked and an eerie silence hung about the store. At first, we silently admired the bread and the cookies grandly displayed behind the window pane. But after standing quietly for a few minutes, Marieke suddenly began to whisper hoarsely.

"There were airplanes early this morning, Linnet. I heard them. It was like a loud buzzing – like giant bees. I looked out of the window and there were a lot of planes flying over our house."

Although I heard her words, I was not really listening but was wondering where the lady was who usually helped me in the bake shop. After Marieke's loud whisper, I banged on the door.

"Hello. Is anyone there?" No one answered, and Marieke pulled me away.

"I want to go home now, Linnet. I ran away because my *Mem* was crying at breakfast and my *heit* was angry."

"Well," I answered rather doubtfully, "I suppose I can walk you home and then come back here again. It's a little early after all."

"Yes, please walk home with me," Marieke replied.

Marieke and her *Mem* and *Heit* lived at the western end of the village. They rented a cottage like ours, but unlike ours, it was not a cottage concealed in the dunes but stood in a field. It took about fifteen minutes to get there. We passed through the village with its quaint, A–shaped, roofed houses. A number of people were about, most standing in their doorways chatting quietly, and some holding their hands above their eyes scanning the sky. But no one said "Hello," or "Isn't it a fine morning?" as they were wont to do on other days. We followed a winding, sandy path out of the village, and Marieke eventually pointed out the red–slated shingles of a small dwelling.

"That's our house," she said, and letting go of my hand, began to run towards it. Following at a slower pace, I watched her open the gate of a rather dilapidated, picket fence and sprint towards the front door. Then she was gone.

I stood and observed for a moment, but she did not reappear.

As I plodded back through town a bit later, I did see more of people. Groups were now bunched together on their lawns, tiny crowds had gathered in clumps under trees, and two or three groups of people clustered by the side of the road engaged in subdued conversations. Retracing my steps to the bakery, I once again knocked. But nothing had altered. Through the window I could ascertain that the shop was still empty. Perhaps the baker and his wife were out among the people I had seen on the street. Beginning to feel uncomfortable, I left off knocking on the door and made for home. Looking up at the sky, I could not detect any airplanes. Perhaps Freddy and Thea would know what the problem was.

"Where have you been?" Thea demanded, embracing and simultaneously shaking me in her anger, the moment I walked in.

I caught Freddy's eye. He was sitting on the couch in a corner of the living room. He put his finger on his lips, and I took that to mean I was not to speak of *boterkoek*.

"I was out walking," I said, "and met Marieke. She says there is war, even though Mr. De Geer said there would not be war."

Thea let go of my shoulders and turned around to face Freddy. I went on.

"Marieke says she heard airplanes early this morning. She said they sounded like buzzing bees. Her *Heit* and *Mem* are going to move away from the island."

Thea walked over to Freddy and sat down next to him. Then she beckoned with her hand that I should come and sit by them as well. I took off my coat and hung it over a chair before I sat down between them. Freddy cleared his throat.

"We might be moving too, Little Thing. We're not sure yet."

"But is there war, Freddy?" I asked, leaning my head against his shoulder. "I didn't see anyone fighting in the village, but lots of people were outside talking together. But there was no one in the bakery . . . ."

I stopped suddenly. Now I had given it away.

"The bakery?" Thea immediately asked, "What were you doing at the bakery, Linnet?"

"Nothing," I said, turning red with shame that I had perhaps revealed the surprise that Freddy had arranged.

"Nothing?" Thea retorted. "That can't be true, Linnet."

Freddy stepped into the conversation. His voice was steady and reassuring. "She went there because I asked her to go. It's your birthday after all, Thea. I thought that a nice cake would do fine to-day."

Thea began to cry. "Oh, Freddy, and here I thought with all these things going on that you had forgotten all about my birthday. I wasn't going to say anything about it, because it doesn't matter really."

Freddy lifted me to his other side and took Thea in his arms.

"There, there now," he crooned. "Of course, I wouldn't forget. How could I forget with you turning thirty–seven, a most important year? And me with a wonderful present hidden away for you too."

Thea wiggled out of his arms and sat up straight. "A present besides the *boterkoek*?"

"Yes. It's not much, but I think you might like it."

I sat up too and wondered what it was. Freddy had not told me about another present. With visible effort, he heaved his long body off the couch, smiled at us, and went upstairs. Thea looked at me.

"Sorry, Little Thing. I'm truly sorry I got angry. It's just that I was so worried about you and what, with the news on the radio that we are at war after all, in spite of what Mr. de Geer said."

"He's a dreadful liar, isn't he, Thea?"

Freddy raced down the stairs at a fast clip. He bumped straight into my words, holding a package covered in brown paper. Bringing it to Thea, he placed it into her hands.

"Here you are, woman of my dreams. This is a gift just for you, and I hope you like it."

I myself had nothing to give Thea but a little poem, and I felt slightly guilty. Thea began fumbling at the brown wrapping. Eventually something red fell out of the package, something silken and red. It was a very fine, long and flowing scarf. Thea cried out in delight. "Oh, Freddy. It's beautiful!"

"Put it on, Thea," I said. "Put it on so we can see how it looks on you."

Smilingly she draped it over her shoulders and stood up. Smooth and lightweight, it embraced her and then let go, fluttering about her form like a butterfly.

"You look just beautiful, Thea," I breathed, "just like a fairy queen. And can I give you a present now too, Thea – one that I made?"

"You made me a present?" Thea's voice and eyes were filled with amazement.

"Yes, but it's just something I made. I have to get it."

I raced upstairs, my feet thudding on the wood, took a crumpled piece of paper out from under my pillow, and ran down again.

"Here," I said, as I presented her with the rather grubby paper, a paper which had been the subject of erasion a thousand times, "I wrote this for you."

Thea read out loud:

"A little finch was in a box
On the shore of a ditch
Her name was Linnet
She was poor and not rich,
But Thea found her

And did not want her to roam,
She took her to Freddy and made her a home."

Thea's voice quavered when she read. In spite of the quavering, she did read the poem beautifully, and I was quite proud of myself. It had been a literary endeavor of some weeks. Every night, I had pondered what would rhyme with ditch, or box, or Linnet. It had been very tricky.

"Oh, Linnet," Thea said, "I love this poem, and I will keep it always."

"And when you wear the scarf and dance, will you sing the words?" I demanded.

"Yes," she laughed, "I surely will."

4

It was only five days after this that I heard Thea cry in a most hopeless fashion in the large bedroom. The sound made me afraid, and I trudged up the stairs rather timidly. I knew that she didn't like me to know when she was feeling sad. But Freddy had gone out, and I did so want to comfort her, because the sobbing was so forlorn. Peeking around the corner, I saw that Belle was sitting on the bed contemplating with big green eyes the weeping figure of her mistress. I pretended that I was looking for Belle and called out, "Belle, Belle," with a loud voice.

Thea sat up, not even bothering to wipe her eyes, although she did produce a handkerchief from her apron pocket with her left hand. "Linnet!" her hoarse voice questioned, "Weren't you supposed to go out with Freddy?"

"Yes, but he told me to go home again because he was meeting someone."

"Oh."

Thea swung her feet over the edge of the bed, sat up, and stared at me. Her shoulders were hunched over, and she stared and stared, but I knew that she did not really see me.

"What's the matter, Thea?" I almost whispered, not knowing if I really wanted to know what was the matter. I just wanted Thea to be happy and to smile.

"The matter?" she responded. "The matter is that a city is burning, Linnet – a city is on fire." More tears sprang into her eyes as she spoke and she crumpled the handkerchief in her hands – hands which had turned into fists."

"Burning?" I said, "A city? What city, Thea?"

"The city where some of my friends live," she answered, "the city of Rotterdam. Listening to the news, as I did just now, I think that they must be dead. Because it sounds like the neighborhood where they lived is totally destroyed."

The truth was that I did not know that Thea had friends in another city. She had never told me. The truth was that I had never really thought about such a possibility. There had always just been Freddy, Thea, and myself. Maybe Freddy had friends, or a mother and a father in another city too. I imagined flames, in my head. I had never really seen a fire before, except when we sometimes made a little one on the beach out of driftwood, when we sat watching the sea at night and waiting for rabbits to come out. I imagined the village of Schiermonnikoog burning. That would be a very big fire. Thea moaned softly. I walked over and sat down next to her, putting my arms about her waist.

"I'm sorry, Thea," I whispered. "What were your friends' names?"

"Cor and Anna," she whispered back, "Cor and Anna."

"Oh."

"And we have capitulated to the Germans, Linnet."

"Capitulated?"

"Surrendered, Linnet. We have lost. We had hardly begun to fight, but we lost already."

"Oh."

She stroked my arms and then said, "I think I will lie down for a while now, Little Thing. I think I'm very, very tired."

"All right, Thea."

She lay down, and I made sure that she was totally covered by the blankets and tucked her in very carefully, even as she did me every night. Then I kissed her on the cheek, breathing into her ear the same three words that she breathed into mine each evening. "I love you."

There seemed nothing left to accomplish, so I retired to the kitchen. Freddy was gone, and I could not ask him what to do. Maybe I could go for a walk into town and find him. Perhaps someone there might tell me about the burning city.

It was on that exact same day, the day of Thea's heartache, that the German soldiers began to occupy the island. Freddy later told me that they had crossed over from the nearby Frisian island of Borkum. Wearing high leather boots, they marched through the village of Schiermonnikoog – marched two by two in gray–green uniforms. There were thirty of them. I counted carefully as I stood among the islanders who were congregating in groups on either side of the main road. The soldiers didn't smile and looked neither to the right nor the left. But their solemn faces didn't deter a little island girl from trotting over to one of the advancing soldiers and trustfully trying to slip a pudgy right hand into his. Her mother immediately stepped out from a small group, scolding as she came, taking the girl by the left hand and pulling her away. I kept a close watch on the soldiers as they paced through the Prins Bernhardweg in the village. I wanted to make sure they were not going to start a fire somewhere. Most of them were Freddy's age or younger. In spite of my trepidation regarding their presence, I greatly admired their uniforms. I could not believe the number of pockets gracing the jackets. My own jacket only sported two pockets and these were often filled to the brim with shells, leaves, feathers and flowers. To have a jacket that was actually embellished with four pockets seemed to me to be the height of luxury. Two pockets were set on their chests and two were situated near the base of the gray–green jackets. I wondered if the pockets held matches for fire, concurrently pondering if Thea could make me such a jacket? But Thea was not fond of Germans and was not likely to want to copy their uniforms.

I suddenly noticed to my amazement that the soldiers had two pockets in their pants as well. These pockets ran along the side of their legs. Thea permitted me to wear pants sometimes in the fall and in the winter, but mostly she made me wear either a dress or a skirt. My pants were blue, not green, and they were puff pants with elastic on the bottom by my ankles. But they held not one single pocket. It made me ponder the advantage of being a soldier. After the formation disappeared down the road, I tried to kick my right leg into the air even as all the soldiers had been doing in unison. It looked extremely simple, but I almost fell over trying. Effortlessly, they strode along, and I watched their retreating, straight backs with a certain degree of envy.

Surveying the now–empty road, I continued in my imitation of their strange marching, until Freddy tapped me on the back. "Doing the goose step, Little Thing? And what are you doing here anyway?"

Ignoring the second question, I said, "You mean the Brant goose, Freddy?"

He laughed. "I don't think the Brant goose walks like that. There's literally no comparison, Linnet. Have you ever seen a Brant goose, or any goose for that matter, walk like these soldiers?"

I shook my head and giggled. Indeed, I had never seen any birds amble about in unison in such a way that resembled these German soldiers. Geese waddled, and the Brant goose in particular walked with short steps and swayed as it walked.

"Maybe," Freddy proffered his wisdom, "it is called the goose step because it makes the soldier who walks in such a way look as silly as a goose."

I laughed again.

"Or maybe," he added, "it is because geese often stand on one leg, and that is what the soldiers seem to do for a moment when they march like that."

"You are so smart, Freddy," I said, and really believed he was. But then I added a fib. "And I wasn't afraid of them either. Why should I be, if they're as silly as geese?"

"Indeed," he answered, "why should we be afraid?"

"Thea is afraid, Freddy," I soberly stated, "and she was crying on the bed. But she might be sleeping now."

"Crying?"

"She says she listened to the radio, and then she told me that she has friends in a city which burned down."

Freddy took my hand and began to run back towards our home, towards our little cottage.

"Is it true, Freddy?" I panted as I ran next to him. "Did a city burn down, and does Thea have friends who were burned in it?"

"Yes," he replied, not stopping at all. "Yes, Linnet, it is true about the city. I heard it when I was speaking with my friend. I never expected, no one did, that the Germans would bomb Rotterdam. I should have come back to the cottage right away."

"Do you have friends there too, Freddy?"

"No," he puffed, "not there, Linnet. But I do have family and friends in other places."

"Where, Freddy?"

He did not answer, but just pulled me along.

"Ow, Freddy, you're hurting my arm."

He stopped then and ruefully looked down at me.

"I'm sorry, Linnet. But I shouldn't have left Thea alone. I had to speak to someone though. It was very important and I couldn't put it off."

"Who did you have to speak to, Freddy?"

"A friend, Little Thing, and a very good friend at that. I will tell you about it this evening."

We began walking again, but it was at a slower pace, and I could see our cottage in the distance. It was mild out, and a rabbit scurried away into the dunes right in front of our feet. A cat could kill a rabbit. Freddy had told me that Belle would be able to kill a rabbit, and that's why we kept her well–fed. I loved rabbits, and often Freddy, Thea, and I would see dozens on the nights that they took me rabbit watching. Freddy said that you saw more if you went out when the moon was full.

I wondered if Thea was still crying. When rabbits are lonely, Freddy had told me, they made crying noises. But they never had tears. Thea had a lot of tears, and her handkerchief was all crumpled and wet. Rabbits did not have handkerchiefs, and they had no pockets either.

"Linnet, we're here."

Freddy let go of my hand and hastened up our small stone path. He stopped at the door, turned, and smiled at me. I smiled back.

"Linnet, do you think you could make us a cup of tea?"

"Oh, yes," I breathed deeply, "I can, Freddy. And I'll put in some extra sugar for Thea."

He beamed at me.

"Good girl, Linnet. Now just wait until I call you up or until I come downstairs."

Alone in the kitchen, I contemplated the fact that I loved making tea. Thea did not let me handle tea cups very often. She said making tea was her job and that she was always both pleased and thankful to serve Freddy and myself. I checked the cupboard to see if there were cookies to go along with the tea. A small box of *speculaas*, spice cookies, said hello to me, and feeling very grownup, I opened that box and took out three. Then, weighing the matter carefully in my mind, I put six out on a plate. It was a solemn day, after all, and two of the spicy, crisp cookies would certainly be good for Thea.

Almost twenty minutes later, Freddy called from upstairs. "Linnet, how's the tea coming?" It made me sound so adult, so grown-up, that I reached for one of Thea's aprons.

"I'm ready, Freddy, and I'll be right up."

After tying the waistband of the red apron behind my back, I deposited the tea cups and saucers and the plate of cookies on a tray and slowly managed to walk up the stairs without spilling even a little bit. To my relief, Thea was sitting up in bed, pillows behind her back, looking quite normal, while Freddy lounged on the edge. They both smiled at me.

"Oh, Linnet," Thea murmured, looking at the tray, "that's a lovely tea."

After painstakingly serving both Freddy and Thea, I set the tray on the little night table next to the bed. Taking my own cup in hand and laying two cookies on the edge of its saucer, I sat down. Then I dipped my *speculaas* into the clear red liquid and swished it about gently to make it wonderfully soggy. They tasted the best that way. Thea stirred her tea thoroughly, as I had told her I put lots of sugar into the bottom of her cup.

When he was done with his drink, Freddy stroked Thea's back before turning to me. I was sitting on a little chair, a chair which Freddy had built especially for me and which always stood in their bedroom.

"Well, Little Thing, it's time for a talk. You've heard what Thea told you, that Holland is now officially at war with Germany, and we, Thea and I, have decided that now is the time to leave the island."

"Leave the island?"

I was incredulous. There had been the talk about hiding, but leaving was something else. When you hid, eventually you came out again, but when you left, well, you might not come back.

"Yes," Freddy went on, "remember that I told you that war is a nasty thing. As matters stand, Schiermonnikoog is German, is being occupied by Germans, and we are currently actually living in enemy territory. I imagine that presently, at the beginning of their stay, the

Germans will try to be friendly. But the truth is that we will be prisoners and I will most likely be sent to work in Germany for them. Or," he went on somberly, "I will be made to build bunkers on the island to help fortify it."

I did not follow everything. I did not know what a bunker was, but the word sounded fearfully ominous. I was too upset to ask. My mind was in a turmoil. I now understood why Marieke had been crying. How could we leave the island – a place we loved so much? Perhaps the Germans would let us live here without asking Freddy to work for them. I said as much, but both Thea and Freddy shook their heads.

"No, Linnet. In retrospect, the German soldiers have not been hospitable to the countries they have taken over. They have camps for people they do not like. They have guns. They have plans to win the war, and they do not want to do us any favors."

"Well," I said, tears in my voice, for I was totally surprised by all this information, even though Freddy had hinted about the hiding. "Where will we go?"

"To the mainland, to some people whom we know and who will take us in. Perhaps some family that I have."

"What people? What family? And," I added irrelevantly, "will there be birds?"

"There are always birds, Linnet," Thea answered, "and you will see them no matter where you are."

"We will be leaving in about three weeks' time," Freddy soothed. "I think we will be safe until that time. And if it seems to me that things are not safe, why, then we will leave earlier. It will give us time to pack and time to carry some of our belongings away."

"Will we see Marieke again?"

"No, I don't think so, Linnet."

5

The soldiers began building a village on the east side of the island at the end of the Prins Bernhardweg. Still a little distance from where we lived, it began to be called *Schleidorp*, Schlei village, by the people in Schiermonnikoog. There were only the islanders and the soldiers on the island now. Even though it was well–nigh summer, tourists were no longer allowed to frequent our beach or rent a cottage. Without a special pass, not a soul from the mainland was allowed to visit nor was anyone allowed to leave.

"Are we going to stay on the island much longer, Freddy?" I asked as we were walking along the beach about two weeks later.

We weren't permitted to go very far towards the eastern side of the coast, as that was the side occupied by many of the increasing number of soldiers. Actually, we were technically not authorized to walk the beach at all. But the east side was where our cottage was and our familiar beach beckoned us. Besides that, staying in and around the village perimeter proved to be a dreadfully difficult for

Freddy. Before long he had developed a bad case of cabin fever. The soldiers had been on the island for about ten days.

"We will be leaving soon, Linnet," he answered me in a low voice.

"Where will we go, Freddy?"

"To the mainland."

"Will we go on the ferry?"

Sauntering slowly as we were speaking, I suddenly stopped dead in my tracks, for I saw something lying on the sand a stretch of some thirty feet up from where we were. It was not a seal and certainly was not a jellyfish.

"Freddy," I pointed, "Look!!"

He stopped and shading his eyes with his right hand, stared where I had indicated.

"What is it, Freddy?"

"It's a person, Linnet. Someone who has drowned. I want you to . . . ." He broke off his words. After we stood quietly for a moment, I was able to discern the form better. The body's face was turned away from us. But it was a soldier. I could tell by the uniform.

"We won't go any closer, Linnet. The fellow is dead. I think we better go home. The man will be found by the soldiers sooner or later and we don't want to be the ones to tell them. I'd rather they weren't familiar with my face."

We turned sideways, retreating towards the dunes. Freddy virtually knew every inch of the island, and we soon found ourselves on a path leading back to our cottage.

"Who was the drowned person, Freddy?"

"I don't know, Linnet. It might have been a pilot. There has been a lot of air combat going on. Planes are shot down into the water and bodies have been coughed up by the sea here and on the other islands around us. It also might be a soldier shot and killed at a battle at a French seaport, a seaport called Dunkirk. That's a battle that is ongoing right now."

"Right now this very minute?"

"Yes."

"So the dead man was a soldier?"

"I'm afraid it might be so, Linnet. He is most likely a victim from the battle I just mentioned, Dunkirk. Thea and I have heard on the radio that many French and British soldiers who fought there have lost their lives. The bodies of many men will be . . . ."

He stopped.

I pulled at his hand.

"It's all right, Freddy. I know it will be all right. The Germans will find the man on the beach and they will bury him in our cemetery for sailors."

We had a graveyard on the island called *Vredenhof*. It was very nice cemetery and sometimes I went and sat in it because it was so quiet. Rabbits and birds liked it too and now and then Freddy and I would sit on the grass at the side of the white gravestones and do some birdwatching. But only the bodies of those who had been washed up on the shores of the island could be buried there. The first grave in the cemetery dated back to 1906, Freddy had told me. That was a long time before I was born. It used to be, Freddy had told me as well, that the hundreds of sailors who had washed ashore on Schiermonnikoog over many years had been buried at the foot of the dunes. This was much too close to the sea, he recounted, and after a bad storm their bodies were often unearthed again. So the islanders asked the count if they could set aside a piece of the island for a cemetery and he told them that would be fine.

"Yes," Freddy answered, "I'm sure that the man we saw on the beach will be buried in the cemetery, Linnet. But I feel that I should be fighting too, fighting for our country. There are so many men fighting and dying and I'm here doing nothing."

He suddenly knelt down and took me into his arms. "Little girl," he said, "I don't ever want you to think that I am a coward."

"Oh, I don't think you are, Freddy," I answered, "You are strong and brave. You always swim the farthest from shore and you carry me all the time. I love you so much, Freddy."

"I love you too, Little Thing. But please remember . . ." he stopped for a moment before he went on, "Please remember that I might not always be there for you. I might have to do things which would take me away from you."

"What, Freddy? What would you have to do?"

"I might have to fight, Linnet."

Men from the island began to be conscripted into helping to build the fortifications the soldiers were beginning on the northeastern side. Working on the island close to their homes seemed better to most of the islanders than being shipped away from their families to a forced labor camp somewhere in far–away Germany. The Germans, who seemed to be friendly, even paid for the labor. Consequently, since tourism had disappeared from the island, the bitter toil for the enemy had its compensations. Thereupon, the drudgery and sweaty work on bunkers, barracks, all sorts of anti–aircraft artillery and radar installations started in earnest – started even as the German flag, the swastika, waved in the wind near the red lighthouse.

As the island now rapidly evolved into a coastal defence area, more and more of Schiermonnikoog became restricted and off–limits to its local inhabitants. German sailors, the *Kriegsmarine*, moved into the north–western part of the island, whereas our eastern side was beginning to be occupied with pilots, the *Luftwaffe*.

It was only a few days after we had spotted the body on the beach that Freddy and Thea told me we would be leaving the island in the evening of the next day.

"Where are we going?" I asked again, only to be answered once more that we were heading for the mainland.

The mainland was large. It contained many places, places about which Freddy and Thea rarely spoke, and for that reason I knew very little about them. It made me slightly nervous to move to an unknown region, but at the same time it also aroused my curiosity. Thea, since that day I had found her weeping so bitterly, had transformed into a very quiet person. Even when she tucked me into bed at night, she did so with as few words as possible. But sometimes I would catch her looking at me in a pensive, solemn and wistful way. It was such a way that made me want to hug her, that made me want to take her insides out and read them so that I could understand what she was thinking and what she was needing. These were the times that I would climb out of my cot and whisper into her ear before she could whisper into mine.

"I love you, Thea. I love you so much."

On the afternoon of our departure, Thea told me I would have to wear two sets of clothes – one right overtop of another. My blue pants would go over top of a blue skirt. I reckoned that it would not be very comfortable. She conceded that it might be a little bulky for me but Freddy had only been able to take so many clothes with him to the mainland on the trips in which he had managed to venture clear of the island. As a matter of fact, she had continued, we probably have to leave a number of things behind.

"Why can't we just come back for them, Thea?"

"Because we can't, Linnet. We just can't. You see, Little Thing, we won't be coming back for a while – for quite a while."

"How long is quite a while, Thea? Is it a week? Or two weeks? Or is it until a birthday?"

"Linnet, don't ask so many questions. We'll just take it one day at a time."

"Are we going to go with the ferry?"

"I think that all you have to know right now is that you will travel with us, Sweet Thing. That way, if anyone asks you before this evening, you won't know how or where."

"Oh."

"Now run along. Play outside for a little while. I've got a number of things to do before we leave. Be sure not to go too far. Stay around the house and be sure to be back by tea time. Promise, Linnet?"

"Yes, Thea."

I ambled off through the back door and stayed in our little yard for a spell. Peering out at the dunes and listening to the waves, I began to feel sad. These were such good sights and sounds. If we were not coming back for a long time, perhaps I should collect some souvenirs, some lovely island keepsakes through which we might remember the sea and the dunes. Maybe I could collect a few periwinkles. I loved the small, snail–like creatures who always hid inside their little black shells. Maybe I could track down some shallow rockpools before tea time, because rockpools were where the periwinkles frequently gathered in piles. I had often collected them with both Freddy and Thea. Seaweed and other sea creatures settled on the bottom of these pools and we had spent a lot of time peering and gazing down into them because the periwinkles liked to conceal themselves under the seaweed. They were black and very hard to find. A certain amount of courage was needed when to thrust your hands down through the algae to locate periwinkles. But when the hard, rounded shells were brought up and washed in the pool water to make sure they were periwinkles, there was satisfaction. It was an enjoyable pastime, and there had been days when the three of us had collected enough to eat for a good snack.

Thea washed the periwinkles with pump water and cooked them in a pot for about five minutes, adding a little salt. Draining the pan, she would set it on the table so that Freddy and I could sit down for a feed. It was so much fun to scoop the snails onto our plates, stab inside the shells with a little fork, and remove the meat. Tasting mighty good, sweet and salty at the same time, I began to salivate just thinking of it.

Of course, if I collected a few periwinkles now, we wouldn't eat them today, but I could keep them in my pocket for a memento. They would dry and then, after we had settled in a different place, I could take them out and look at them, remembering how we'd had great fun. It was a good idea.

I bimbled off toward the path we always took towards the west beach, next to the wide, wide strand we so loved. Taking care to walk between the outlying dunes, I kept a sharp lookout for any

soldiers that might be patrolling the beach. There had been a grow-
ing number of them. In the faint distance behind me I could make
out some figures, but they were quite, quite far away. And if I could
hardly see them, surely they could not see me. Was I not a lot
smaller? This is what I reasoned.

There were white caps on the sea. I had asked Freddy why they
were called white caps and not white hats. Hats are common, he had
replied, but caps, well, caps are out of the ordinary, Linnet. Not
many people wear caps, but everyone wears a hat. I didn't know if
he was speaking the truth at that point. There were, after all, many
islanders who wore caps.

I walked towards the west. Freddy had said the west beaches
were less patrolled. Making for an area where I knew there were
rock pools, I kept away from the open beach. Rock pools were natu-
ral hollows in coastal rocks, hollows which filled with water each
day as the tide rose. I half crouched and half walked as I went. Intent
and focused upon reaching my destination, I was totally bewildered
when I tripped over a pair of legs sticking out of a dune depression
and landed face down in the sand. The legs over which I had tripped
were gray–green and they had pockets.

"Hello."

The voice which belonged with the legs was rather deep, but
not at all frightening. Hands took hold of the back of my jacket and
pulled me upright. Then they turned me. A friendly pair of blue
eyes, darker blue than Freddy's, smiled down into mine.

"*Wie gehts?*"

I could not quite make out the German words, but its questioning and interested tone was reminiscent of how I had spoken to
Marieke when I had found her sobbing. I brushed some sand

granules off my cheeks. The soldier, for that is what the uniform I was staring at covered, a real German soldier, took a handkerchief out of one of his pockets.

"Here, *Mädchen*. This will help you."

I took the handkerchief and wiped my eyes. And then I found my voice.

"Thank you, Sir."

He grinned. "That is very *höflich* of you to say. It is my *vergnügen* to help such a beautiful, young lady."

He made me grin and in that one moment made me forget that he was an enemy, that he was fighting our country. Although his Dutch was marked with a heavy accent, his speech was very clear and I understood almost all of what he was saying.

"What brings you out on this lovely day?"

"I'm looking for periwinkles."

I could not see any reason why I should not tell him this. After all, what reason could he have to fight periwinkles?

"Periwinkles?"

He repeated the word slowly as if tasting it, and I understood that this word was a difficult one. So I tried to help him.

"You know, snails."

"Ah, snails. Yes, *Schnecke*. I know snails. *Strandschnecke*, I think."

I had no idea if that was correct. His guttural interpretation sounded foreign to me, but if he thought he knew what periwinkles were, that was fine by me.

"So you look for these snails on the beach?"

"Well," I enlightened him, still brushing my face with his handkerchief, "actually I was looking for rock pools, because that is where they usually are."

I handed him back his handkerchief and with my hands began brushing off my blue pants – my puff pants without any pockets.

"I like all your pockets. You have a lot of pockets." The words came out of my mouth spontaneously and the soldier smiled broadly, sitting back down in the sand.

"*Ja, die Taschen*. You like pockets?"

"Oh, yes," I breathed, "pockets are wonderful. You can carry feathers, shells, leaves, and all sorts of things that you find."

"I have something special in one of my pockets," he said, "but before I show you, you must tell me your name and I will tell you mine. Mine is Jůrgen."

"Jůrgen," I repeated, and again, "Jůrgen."

"*Ja*," he said and smiled again, showing a mouthful of white, strong teeth.

"My name is . . . ," I hesitated.

Would it be all right to tell him my name? What if he came look-ing for me and found Freddy and took him away to work on the bunkers. I could hear Freddy say, "*You shouldn't have told him your name, Linnet. We are running away from the island.*" Running away meant . . . well, it meant that someone was chasing you. I gave Jůrgen another look from under my eyelashes. He was still smiling and studying me with a mixture of confidence and hope.

"My name is Emma," I blurted out.

It was a name I liked, and recently Freddy had told me a story about a dog whose name was Emma. Surely it would be safe to use.

"Emma," Jůrgen slowly repeated, and again, "Emma. Well, you will not believe this, but I have a . . . ."

He stopped and reached into a pocket in the back of his pants, a pocket I didn't even know he had. Taking out a flat, brown wallet and unfolding it, he carefully extracted a photograph. Staring at it for a long moment, he then shifted his gaze to me and crooked the pinkie of his right hand to tell me to step over. I did, and he lowered the photograph so that I could see what was on it.

"This is *mein kleiner Màdchen. Sie heisst Emma.*"

I was confronted with the picture of a girl, a girl who looked to be my age, standing by a wooden, high–backed chair. She had long, blond hair which was tied back with a large, blue ribbon. Her hand rested on the arm of the chair. The tiniest of smiles animated her face just a bit, and she wore a very clean, white apron over a dark dress.

"She is very pretty," I said, "I think her ribbon is lovely. Sometimes my Thea . . ." I stopped, abruptly glancing up at Jûrgen, but he did not react at all to my mentioning Thea. He was running his thumb over the picture.

"*Ja,*" he agreed, "she is *süss.*"

"How old is she?"

"She is five," he responded rather proudly, "and she sings like a *Nachtigal.*"

"Nightingale?"

"*Ja,* " he repeated proudly, "like a nightingale."

"Nightingale – luscinia, luscinia," I automatically replied, "I have never heard a nightingale sing, and I have never even seen one. But I have seen a warbler. They sing nicely too."

"A warbler?"

"Yes," I was eager to show off what I knew, "they are fat little birds with round heads, grey with brown eyes, and the species is *sylvia borin.*"

I stopped. Was I giving him too much information again?

"You are *kenntnisreich,* Emma."

I blushed. Not because of whatever he so kindly had said, but because I deeply realized within myself that neither Freddy nor Thea would approve of me bragging in front of a German soldier or, for that matter, bragging in front of anyone. Jûrgen slowly inserted the photograph of his daughter back into his wallet and returned it to his back pocket.

"It was a nice picture."

He smiled. It was a rather dejected smile. And then he softly spoke. "God has given me a *ein wunderbare Familie*."

I understood the world family clearly. And I understood that it had been given to him by someone.

"God?" I asked.

"*Ja, der gute Gott,*" he repeated,

Red cabbage leaves, ditches, boxes and question marks swam through my head. Was God perhaps someone like the German count? Was he a nice man, a man like the count who had owned the island? Could He give away families at will? I did not understand. So I probed.

"Does God know the Count? You know the Count who owns the island?"

He regarded me quizzically.

"What do you mean?"

"I mean, who is God?"

"You do not know who God is?"

"No."

From the way Jûrgen accentuated every word in his sentence, it became clear to me that God was very important to him and that he thought it was very stupid of me not to know who He was. Perhaps God would turn out to be the other little German man about whom Freddy had told me; the man who Freddy had said was not very good; and the man who wanted to fight and take homes away from people. But Jürgen had just said that he had received his family from this man.

"Is God German?" I blurted out.

If anything, Jürgen's expression became more puzzled and he sat down on the sand.

"God," he spoke quietly and very slowly, "is the Maker of everything, *kleines Màdchen,* of everything in the whole world. *In der Tat,* He made everything you now see around you. And He always takes care of me because He is always with me."

It took a moment for me to realize the enormity of what Jürgen had just said. I heard the waves behind me grow taller as they approached the island shore, and I heard them topple down into long breakers. I felt the wide sky above me, so wide that they could not fill my eyes when I gazed up, and I saw all the grains of sand at my feet, so many I could not count them.

"He made everything?" I repeated.

He nodded.

"Niemand has told you this?"

I shook my head. Neither Freddy nor Thea had ever talked about God. Maybe they didn't know Him either. "Do all the Germans know God?" I asked.

He smiled wryly, rubbing his hands together. Freddy did that too.

"Some do," he answered me, "but many don't."

"How did you find out about Him? Does He live nearby your house in Germany?"

"He lives in my house, *ja,* " Jürgen answered, "and He can live in yours too if you want Him to."

72

It was the strangest conversation I had ever had. For although I was only five years old, I knew for a fact that someone could only live in one place at a time. Hadn't I heard Freddy say a thousand times, *Go and bother Thea, Linnet. I can't play with you right now. I have to be at my bird watching post. Don't you know I can't be in two places at the same time.*

"He can live at my house and at yours at the same time?" I asked just to confirm what I thought had said.

"*Ja,* He surely can."

"How can He do that?"

"Well, Emma, I can't answer that. You see I don't know. But what I do know is that He can."

I stared at him. He sat in the sand in the grey–green uniform with the myriad pockets, but what he carried in his mind interested me more than the pockets right now. I could sense that what he said was true because . . . . well, actually didn't know why I thought that what he said was true, but I knew within myself that it was.

"Is it important, Jûrgen?"

"It is *sehr wichtig,* Emma."

"How do you know it is true, Jûrgen?"

"Because I read of it in *die Bibel.*

"Is that a book?"

"It is *das Buch der Bûcher.*"

"I have never read it."

"There is a church in the village, I think," Jûrgen opted. "You can go there and you will hear the Bible read."

I knew the word church. I knew it was the name of the building in the village with the steeple tower. That tower was not half as big as the Fire Tower, but it always pleased me to look at it when I passed it. It was a sort of mother building to all the houses on the street. Certainly it was the largest structure in the village, and with the church cemetery wrapped around it, was a very peaceful place. Of course, I couldn't tell Jûrgen that I couldn't go to the church any time soon, because we were leaving the island that evening. And then I remembered that I had promised to be back by tea time, and that if I wasn't, Thea would be very cross with me.

"It is kind of you to tell me," I responded, "and I will try to find a Bible. But I have to go now."

"No *Strandschnecke*, then?" he said with a little laugh.

"Perhaps another time."

I retraced my steps and walked away from him backwards. Would he follow me? But no, he stayed seated in the slip face of the dune, waving as I walked.

"*Auf wiedersehen*, Emma."

"Goodbye, Jûrgen."

As I trudged back through the dunes, taking care to bend down and taking care to avoid crests so that no one might notice me, I wondered that Jûrgen had not asked where my house was. Perhaps he was, after all, following me. At that thought, I immediately turned around to see if he was trailing at my back, but there was nothing behind me other than the salt wind and the hollow imprints of my feet. Should I tell Freddy and Thea about Jûrgen? Instinctively I knew that they would be very upset with the information. Freddy always said when something happened when the two of us were out together that might cause Thea tension or fear, *"Don't upset the apple cart, Linnet. We'll just keep it to ourselves."* Like the time a bull had chased us in a farmer's field and we just barely made it to the fence.

Well, Jürgen could be compared to the bull in the farmer's field, and I certainly didn't want to upset the apple cart.

Thea was standing at the gate when I appeared on the sandy path leading up to the cottage. I could see her face relax into a smile as soon as she saw me, and then her hands beckoned that I hurry. I galloped the last distance, pretending I was a horse, whinnying all the way.

"Good girl, Linnet. I was just starting to get a bit anxious about you. Where were you?"

"Oh, I was just walking about a bit, Thea."

She hugged me.

"Freddy should be back soon. And I have bread all ready to eat. Our plates will be our fists, Little Thing."

"Do you think my stomach is as big as my fist, Thea?"

"Maybe."

"What's on the bread, Thea?"

"Cheese. And now go and wash your hands and face under the pump. After you're all cleaned up, I want you to go upstairs to your room and put on the extra clothes I laid out for you."

"Aw, Thea, can't I wait to do that?"

"No, you can't, Little Thing. Now go on. Do as I say, and take off your jacket first."

I complied, and Thea took my jacket as I dawdled over to the pump. Washing was not a favorite avocation. The metal handle squeaked rustily as I stiffly swung it up and down, up and down. Water gushed out. It was cold, and Belle sat on a garden chair and watched me, her green eyes inscrutable.

"Poor Belle," I sputtered softly, as I splashed the frigid water on my face and rubbed hard, "how will you manage without us? But I think you will catch some mice and perhaps the Germans like cats. I think that Jürgen . . . ."

I stopped abruptly, glancing around to see if Thea had heard what I'd said. But she was nowhere to be seen. Belle blinked. As soon as I had dried my hands on the blue towel hanging on the wooden rack by the door, I ran over to her. Bending down, I stroked her back and scratched behind her ears. She purred generously. Increasing trepidation filled me about leaving her behind, about abandoning our gentle rumbler. How could Thea manage it?! Belle always came to her, frequently slept with her, and always licked her hand and face affectionately. Thea said it felt like rough sandpaper, but that it only meant that the cat loved her.

When I came in, some ten minutes or so later, Thea was not in the kitchen. Dragging my feet up the stairs slowly and quietly, not at all anxious to don two sets of clothes, I found Thea sitting on my cot. She seemed lost in thought and was fingering some black material lying by her side. Curiously I padded over on my stocking feet.

"What is it, Thea?" I asked, pointing to the dark fabric she was stroking.

Startled she looked up at me and then grinned. "You know, Linnet, I was just thinking that I was going to make you disappear."

"Disappear?"

"Yes, disappear into the night. I'm going to make you as dark and as black as the night."

I grinned too.

"How are you going to do that, Thea?"

She held up the black crepe, and I could see that it was a coat of sorts, a long black coat with dark buttons.

"With this cloak, Little Thing. We're going to see how it fits, and I think it will. Tonight we'll be hiking for a long while, and Freddy and I don't want you to be seen by anyone. So you'll be wearing this."

"So, I'll be wearing three outfits then?" I groaned as I spoke and she patted my bum.

"First off, I want you to take off your pants and sweater. Then put on the blouse and jumper on the chair there. After you do that, put your pants and sweater back on overtop of the jumper."

"Thea, I'll be so fat."

"No, you won't be. Now just try."

I did as she said and actually it was not too bad. It was very warm, but I knew it would be chilly out later at night.

"Now," Thea instructed, "put your jacket back on and then slip into this covering overtop of your jacket."

I managed to comply. The black cloak did fit snugly overtop of everything I wore, just as Thea had predicted. But that was not the end of my metamorphosis, for at this point, Thea held up another black creation. It was a hat – a hat with a black veil hanging in front of it. She beckoned me over with her hand, and reluctantly I stood in front of her. The hat neatly embraced my hair but the veil floated darkly in front of my face, prohibiting sight.

"I can't see anything, Thea," I wailed. "How can I ever walk straight with this over my face."

"Just wait, Linnet," Thea soothed, "Just wait."

I did wait and felt Thea carefully nudge the bottom part of the black veil into my jacket collar. She then proceeded to cut two peep-holes into the veil. The openings aligned with my eyes, and I could see again, even though I couldn't see very well.

"How's that?"

"Well," I was a little dubious about the result. "Well, I don't know."

We heard the door slam downstairs and then footsteps pounded up the stairs.

"Hello, girls."

It was Freddy, and he was carrying something. Even though my vision was shrouded, I could make out that two outfits were draped over his arm. Those outfits were gray–green. They had multiple pockets, and I surely wished that I could wear one of them. But the black crepe encompassed me and voided my chances of looking like a soldier.

"Well, girls," Freddy's voice rang out again, "what do you think of these suits?"

My hands reached up to yank off the veil, but Thea was ahead of me.

"Just wait, Linnet. Be careful. It took me a long time to put it all together. I don't want it torn before tonight."

Freddy clucked appreciatively as he eyed my costume. "You look absolutely stunning, Linnet! I don't think anyone will know there's anyone there, and that's exactly how we want it."

"What about you? Everyone will know there's a person inside the uniform."

"Yes," Thea concurred, "and I better put one of them on and see how much too big it is, so I can hem up the pant legs. It'll be way too long for me. But first," and she reached for me, "first we'll take this off until we're ready to leave."

"When," I demanded, even as Thea took off my veil, dark robe, and jacket. "When are we leaving?"

"When it gets dark, Little Thing," Freddy said, "and before that, we will eat, and after we eat, guess who's going to have a nap."

I stuck out my tongue at Freddy and then went to stand by the costumes, admiringly running my hands over the wool and cautiously feeling the inside of the pockets.

"Will you be doing the goose step, Freddy?"

He laughed out loud.

"No, I won't have to, because I won't be marching in a troop, you silly child. But as head gander I will be advancing with the most beautiful mother goose on this whole island – our own Thea. And you will be our little gosling."

"Don't joke about it, Freddy," Thea said, even as she struggled to put on one of the uniforms he had brought, "It's a risky business and we will do well to be sober and to help Linnet see that she must be on guard and very obedient."

Freddy sat down on my cot and patted the place next to him. I sat there and nestled into his side.

"Little Thing," he began, "when we wake you up later tonight, it will be dark outside. It's the best time for us to leave the island, as most people in the village will be asleep and snuggled into their beds. Many of the soldiers will also be sleeping. But there will be some out on patrol."

I listened, only half–absorbing what he said. I understood that we'd be walking in the dark, that we were not to be seen, and that we must be very quiet.

"How are we getting off the island?" I asked.

"Well, there is still sufficient freedom of movement outside the restricted zones," Freddy answered, "for us to foot it a long distance. Later tonight, we'll be getting passage on a boat that will be taking us to the mainland."

"A boat," I repeated. "I've always wanted to go on a boat."

"You might be very tired by the time we get to the boat, Linnet," Freddy told me. "Remember, we'll be walking for a long time."

"Will you carry me, Freddy?"

"That depends," Freddy answered. "If I have to, I will. Now listen carefully, Linnet. You know that we sometimes go on hikes, you and I, and that we look for certain birds. There are times when we just don't see those birds, and then we wait or eventually move to a different spot. Well, it could be that tonight we won't be able to see or find what we've come for and then, well then . . . ."

"What Freddy means," Thea cut in, "is that we might run into a German patrol and that perhaps you'll have to hide, Little Thing. Freddy and I will be wearing uniforms, and that, hopefully, will safeguard us. But you, although we hope no one sees you, are not in uniform. We can't be certain what will happen, and Freddy can't carry you in case we run into a patrol."

"But what if . . . ." I whispered, my heart beginning to beat fast, "what if . . ." and I stopped again.

"No matter what happens, Linnet," Thea reassured me, "we'll take care of you."

But doubts had been sown. How could they take care of me if I had to hide and if they were not with me?

"He is always with me."

I heard Jûrgen's voice, his deep voice as he sat in the dunes looking at me. It was God of whom he had been speaking – the God who could be in two places at the same time. Would He be with me? I must have been dozing off on the cot against Freddy, because the next thing I knew, Freddy was carrying me down the stairs in his big arms and putting me on a chair in the kitchen.

"I want you to eat some bread, Linnet. And after you eat it, I want you to lie down on the couch and try to go to sleep."

I was too sleepy to disagree. There had been no drowsiness in me prior to going upstairs, but now a lassitude settled over me that defied explanation. I ate only half the sandwich before the old sofa nodded me over.

"Linnet! Linnet! Wake up, little girl! It's time to go."

I had no idea how long I had slept, but only knew that there was a deep, deep dark both in and outside the cottage. Freddy and Thea were standing over me. I felt the warm wool of their outfits nudge me as they slowly edged me up. Suddenly aware that I did not have the black robe on, I was overwhelmed with fear.

"Where's my black coat, Thea?" I panicked, "Where is the suit you made me?"

"It's right here, Little One. Don't worry. I'll help you put it on. But I think we might make a little trip to the outhouse first."

When the visit to the privy was finished, Thea guided my arms into the sleeved, black cloak, while we stood next to the pump. Freddy kept an eye on things, rooted next to us like a tree, a green, woolen tree. I thought he looked mighty handsome too, what with a belt buckle that pictured an eagle. As Thea fitted the mantel around me, I told him so.

"Freddy, did you know that you have an eagle on your belt?"

Thea pulled the mask down over my head, so I did not hear his answer. Then she gently tucked the veil into my collar, even as she had done that afternoon.

"Now you are all done, Little Thing, and you are almost invisible."

"Are you ready, Linnet?" Freddy asked, as he held out his hand to me. A cap covered his blond hair. I took his hand and was glad of it, because it was warm and alive and I felt very dark and cold.

"Yes, I am, Freddy."

"Then let's head out."

"Goodbye pump, goodbye Belle, goodbye cottage, goodbye path, goodbye . . . ."

I was hushed by both Freddy and Thea. Then we set out apace, me in the middle. And there was no sound except that of the wind overhead and the waves breaking on the shore.

The sand muffled our steps. Even though we walked side by side, Freddy led the way and carefully marshaled us around the village, not through it. I could understand the reason for it. For what if the baker in the village could not sleep and opened his curtains? If he saw us, he might waken his wife, who was known to be quite a chatterbox. But I surmised that she would not say anything to any-one if she did happen to see us. She was usually very kind. A little later, we briskly passed Marieke's cottage, and I reflected on it. Marieke didn't live there any longer. Where was she? And where would we be after we got to where Freddy was taking us? I squeezed his hand and he squeezed back. But he didn't say a word. I was proud of myself for not speaking either, for speaking was a thing I generally did quite well. Freddy often reminded me of that.

"Be quiet for a little bit, Linnet. The birds will not come if you rattle on so much."

There were no birds out now though. Some animals, Freddy had told me, came out of their hiding places at night, because they felt safer in the dark. These animals were nocturnal. But another group of animals came out at night too, because they liked to hunt and eat nocturnal animals. Nocturnal was a nice word. It meant night. I was not an animal, but I was out at night.

"Lift your feet a little higher, Linnet. You're beginning to drag."

"All right, Freddy."

We were well past Marieke's cottage now. I could not see all that well. My mask was slipping a bit. The holes in the mask for my eyes were not very large and I relied mainly on Freddy's and Thea's hands to pull and direct me forward. Thea's grip on my fingers sud-denly tightened.

"I think I hear someone coming, Freddy."

"To the right into the dunes with Linnet then, Thea."

I felt myself jerked towards the right and I obediently lifted my legs, following as quickly as I could. Thea tugged, and I could feel the sand rise up under my feet into a mound.

"Lie down, Linnet." Thea's voice was tight. I lay down flat and tasted sand. Thea's arm covered my shoulders and I could feel her heart beating against my back. There were footsteps and then a greeting.

"*Kamerad.*"

Freddy's voice answered, "*Kamerad.*"

The footsteps faded. Thea sighed deeply into my back even as I drooled out the sand grains that had slipped beneath my mask. A few moments passed. Then I heard Freddy's whispered command.

"You can come out now, you two. The coast is clear."

We resumed our places next to Freddy. I held onto their hands tightly again. There were no bird calls over us as we walked. I listened carefully. Maybe the birds had heard Freddy say that all must be very quiet, that it was dangerous to speak. I smiled to myself. Birds did not speak, they sang and chirped and made bird sounds. And at this very moment no owl hooted or screeched in the sky above us, and there was no harshly calling moorhen about with its "kek, kek, kek." There were times when I had heard the moorhen call and had seen it too, but that had been during the daytime.

"*Moorhen. What is the species, Linnet?*"

Freddy asked me species questions all the time and I could visualize the words as they magically silhouetted in my mind . . . .

"Gallinula chloropus."

I whispered the term very softly, whispered it into the sound of the surf. It was an especially difficult name to remember.

"*Good girl.*"

Freddy whispered the words into my brain. But I was getting so very tired. We'd been walking a long, long while. My feet began to drag more and more, and no matter that Thea and Freddy pulled me up several times, in the end I could not manage any longer. We stopped and without any conversation, Freddy picked me up and half–slung me over his shoulder. I presumed that with my double layer of clothes under my jacket as well as the black robe, I was quite heavy. Poor Freddy! And then I reckoned that black probably weighed more than blue. It was my last thought before falling soundly asleep.

Sometime later, I was unceremoniously plunked down on some sand, and I awoke with a start. It was still dark, and I shivered. Chilliness enveloped me, but I trembled more with excitement than with cold. I was, at this point, glad of my extra clothes. Blinking a few times, and pulling at my mask to make its holes align with my eyes, I gradually became aware of my surroundings. There was what I perceived to be a boat just steps away, beached in shallow water on the edge of the sea. It was a wooden boat with a rather broad stern. Only some three and a half meters long, it did not ap-pear that it was meant to carry a lot of passengers. A few feet farther, Freddy and Thea were in heavy conversation with a man, presuma-bly the owner of the vessel. I stood up, stood up cautiously, for I did not want to disturb them. Pussyfooting to the boat, I let my hand explore along its edge. There was a steering wheel in the bow. It had eight spokes, all joined at the centre of the wheel. I always admired ships when, standing on the shore, I saw them pass. When the wind blew and the waves crested and troughed, it seemed to me they danced on the water.

"Well, Little Sailor," a low–keyed voice touched my back, "does my boat meet with your approval?"

"Yes," I whispered, fearfully conscious that he spoke quite loud, all too aware of the alleged threat of soldiers behind the dunes.

The voice moved next to me. It belonged to a man who sported a sizeable beard, at least that's what I thought as I peered at him through the dark, and he smiled at me. The white teeth that flashed behind the beard were crooked and gapped, but the smile was friendly enough. I smiled back readily.

"Linnet," Freddy stood next to me now on my other side, "this is Willem. He's going to take us to the mainland."

"It's a good night for crossing," Willem told us. "Calm it is, and there have not been many planes overhead."

I'd forgotten about the planes. It was not just German planes that flew past, Freddy had informed me, but also British ones making for Germany.

"Well, Freddy," Willem rubbed his large hands together as he spoke, "help me push her into the water. And may God protect us in the hours to come."

My ears sharpened. Even as Jürgen, Willem must be acquainted with God. As Thea and Freddy flanked the right side of the craft and Willem shouldered the left, muscling in unison began. As a result, the boat began to slide forward. It moved ahead with a grinding sort of sound. Perhaps, I reasoned, it hurt the sand to have the boat dragged over it. At that moment I was horribly convinced that every single one of the Germans on the whole island would be able to hear us. But the sound lasted only an instant. As soon as the bow hit the water, the awful grating stopped. Freddy came towards me, lifted me up and deposited me into the stern.

"Sit down, Linnet," he whispered, "and stay very still."

Frightfully submissive, I immediately sat down in the spot where Freddy had placed me. One more push and the boat launched further into the water, and I felt the deck move beneath me. Perhaps there were periwinkles and seals and jellyfish all concealed beneath me now. Freddy and Thea joined me in the body of the boat, rocking it from side to side as they jumped in, and finally Willem, giving the vessel a final shove, entered as well. Taking his place behind the reddish–brown steering wheel, he was an impressive, indistinct figure. Wearing a dark slicker he, like the three of us, blended in with the shadows of the night. Faint starlight flickered on the water and the low rumble of the engine was almost negligible. We were moving and I began to relax. Thea reached for my hand and I was glad of it.

Freddy had told me that the distance between Schiermonnikoog and Lauwersoog on mainland Groningen was nine kilometers. But is that where we were going? There had been the odd times when some of Freddy's friends had visited from the mainland, and they had spoken of traveling on the ferry via Ameland, the island next to Schiermonnikoog. They had also mentioned hiking the mudflats – that is, they had used the period of low water tide to wade and walk on the watershed of the mudflats to reach our cottage.

"Where are we going, Thea," I whispered into her ear.

Freddy poked me behind her back. It indicated I was not to speak and I was ashamed, because I had truly promised him I would not say a word. Leaning my head against Thea's side, I fell asleep again.

When I opened my eyes once more, we were nearing a shoreline, presumably the shoreline of the mainland. Willem was idling the boat. It was almost, but not quite, light out and very quiet.

"The water is about waist deep here," Willem stated, "and this is the approximate place where you indicated your friends would meet you. I'll slowly pass up and down the coast for a bit, but I hope your contacts are reliable and not tardy."

"They are," Freddy answered softly, "and I'm sure we'll see them shortly."

I could feel Thea straining her body next to mine as she turned towards the right, towards where the water met the land. I could only see its edge dimly.

"Do not just look for persons," Freddy iterated quietly, "but try to make out something white on the bushes or trees on the shore. It will have been placed there as a sign."

I redoubled my efforts at watching, squinting my eyes. The boat moved forward, inch by inch, towards the bank. Thea sighed. Minutes passed.

"I see something," I whispered, pointing as I spoke. "Over there, Freddy. It's something shiny."

"Where, Linnet?" Freddy answered quietly.

"Where I was pointing, but now it's . . . . No, I see it again! Over there, Freddy!"

I pointed again, my body reacting with an upward motion, causing the boat to sway from side to side.

"Linnet, sit down!"

Thea pulled my black coat and yanked me to a lower position.

"I see it," Freddy mouthed gently. "Yes, that's it. That's where we have to be."

"But there is no one there." Thea spoke in a dispirited manner, and I stroked her uniform. I wondered what they would do with these uniforms. Would they keep them on once we got on shore? It had begun to drizzle, and wet drops ran through my peepholes. My nose was wet.

"Well, I expect that we might have to wait for a bit," Freddy said, as he put his right arm about Thea. "But I'm certain we'll be picked up in this area. Now, Willem, can you get closer to the land, or is that it?"

"Well," Willem responded, "just a mite closer maybe. But not much more."

"When you've reached the limit, let me know and I'll step down into the water. I'll first carry Thea ashore on my back and then come back for Linnet."

Willem grunted and went ahead at a snail's pace.

"That's it, Freddy. If I go any further, I'll beach myself, and although it might be all right, I can't take the chance."

"Fine." Freddy, who had been busy rolling up his gray–green pant legs, first swung his right leg and then his left into the sea. "It's cold," he grinned, and then, "the bottom is firm and that is good. All right, Thea. What stuff are you're made off, my girl? I'm going to turn around. See if you can hop onto my back."

Without a word, Thea stood up. But before she attempted to mount Freddy's broad back, she put out a hand to Willem.

"Thank you, Willem, for risking your life and taking us off the island. That's a wonderful thing you've done."

Willem said nothing in reply as he shook her hand. Then Thea positioned herself so that she could reach out and take hold of Freddy's shoulder. And without any further ado, she jumped onto his back.

"Thea is brave," I told Willem, "and I love her."

"So you should, Little Sailor," he responded gravely. "So you should."

I instinctively felt that I should shake Willem's hand also. So, even as Thea had done, I stretched out my hand towards the captain of the boat.

"Thank you, Sir," I formulated carefully, "for helping us."

His hand was very large and the top of it was hairy. I don't know why I remembered at that point what he had said at the outset of our journey. Thea and Freddy were almost at the shore, so I could speak freely without having to tell them where my thoughts came from. Withdrawing my hand from the skipper's large one, I took a deep breath and launched into my query.

"Willem?" I asked, "is God in this boat?"

If Willem was surprised by my question, he did not let on. "Is God in this boat?" he repeated. "I should say so, child, for you see, God is everywhere."

"Everywhere?"

Much vaster than the information Jürgen had given me earlier the previous day, this intelligence bowled me over. Willem was a grown man, a brave skipper, and he surely knew many things. God, then, was not just at Jürgen's house or in Jürgen's mind, but He was everywhere. I sat motionless and listened to the tiny waves lapping against the stern.

"So, Linnet, are you ready?" Although I had not heard him coming, Freddy was positioned at my side of the boat right next to me, and he had an inviting smile on his face.

"Thea is waiting for you on the shore, Little Thing. But before I freeze to death, and before you climb onto my back, I must shake the hand of our great skipper, Willem."

He proceeded to do so, and then we waded through the water towards Thea, towards land.

7

Once Willem and his boat were out of sight, Freddy divested himself of the uniform. His rolled–up pant legs had crept down. Quite wet, the gray–green wool clung to his limbs. To my surprise, Thea produced a small suitcase from underneath one of the nearby bushes. She opened it and took out some dry pants and a warm sweater for Freddy.

"How did the suitcase get here, Thea?"

"That's for me to know, Linnet."

I knew better than to ask why. Freddy winked at me, took off his wet togs and slipped into the warm clothes. He then folded up his uniform into a sodden, woolen square and set it on the ground.

"There. Now I look like myself again, Little Thing."

Thea took off my hat and mask, as well as my cloak, stowing them with Freddy's clothes. Now I was a color again. Black had transformed me into shade, into something not to be seen. Afterwards, Thea disappeared behind some bushes, reappearing shortly thereafter in a blue dress over which she donned her windbreaker. She, even as Freddy had done, folded up her green pants and jacket.

"What will you do with them?"

"Well, Linnet," Thea answered, "someone will be by later to pick them up. No doubt they will be used by someone else."

"Can't we keep them in case we need them again? What if we have to go back to the island? What if . . . ."

Thea laid a hand on my mouth. "For now you will have to be content, Little Thing, with what we tell you. The less you know the better."

There was a rather stern undertone in her voice.

"Where will we go now?"

The sentence came out rather garbled as Thea's hand still covered my mouth.

"We have to wait," she responded, simultaneously taking away her hand, but chucking a finger under my chin, forcing me to look up into her face, "and we have to wait very quietly. There is a road behind the bushes here, and people might pass by, hear us talking, and wonder where we have come from."

"Yes, Thea," I replied meekly.

So we waited in the drizzle, taking what little protection we could get under trees and bushes. It was quite light now. Slowly we were getting wet and wetter. Could you get wetter once you were wet? The small raindrops hitting the water produced ripples, moving ripples. The surface became almost granular in appearance. Were raindrops round? Or were they flat? There was no doubt that they were drenching me. Drenchdrops – that was a good word! There was a mist rising over the water. I shivered. Within me there rose a mound of loneliness, which I did not understand. After all,

Freddy and Thea were right there next to me. I could hear their very hushed voices as they spoke softly to one another. I was with them, but I was not with them. Not knowing where we were going or how long we would stay here, or what would happen, made me feel isolated. It was as if I were being excluded from a great secret. *"God is everywhere."* Peering through the rapidly rising fog, I wondered what God looked like. But what can you resemble if you are everywhere?

"I think I hear someone coming." Freddy whispered the words tersely, and Thea and I both froze. I could only discern the quiet of the mist, because mist does carry an absence of sound. My breathing was very shallow. Then there was a voice, a muffled voice, rendered through the bushes.

"Freddy? Freddy, are you there?"

Freddy stood up cautiously, answering in a low tone, "Is that you, Jeroen?"

A moment later a man stood in front of us, a tall man, a smiling man and one who immediately made me feel at ease.

"So glad you folks made it. Sorry that I wasn't here to greet the boat but something came up. Better to be safe than sorry."

Freddy and Thea shook hands with Jeroen, who smiled at me as he picked up the uniforms. He then deposited them into a cloth bag.

"Well, if you don't mind a bit of a wait, a car will be along. Then you'll begin the next leg of your journey."

A car? I had never ridden in a car. I had never even seen a car. A sudden impulse to sneeze, not once but three times, shook my body. Thea threw me a concerned look. Freddy walked over.

"Little Thing," he said, "now is the time for me to tell you where we're going."

I nodded and wiped my nose on the back of my hand. Reaching into his back pocket, Freddy produced and handed me a handkerchief before he continued.

"You asked me quite some time ago if I had friends, if I had family. Well, you have this past evening met two of my friends, and in a while you will meet one more and," he stopped for a moment, "later on you will also meet some of my family."

I sat quietly, listening. I did remember that he had mentioned friends and family. It had been after Thea had found out that her friends had probably been killed.

"The chauffeur of the car is another friend you will meet. He is a very good man. He will begin to take us to my home, to where I grew up. But, Little Thing," and here Freddy looked directly into my eyes, "something will happen before you get to my home that you may not like. You see, Thea and I will be leaving before we get there."

"Leaving?" I thought I had not heard Freddy properly and squished his hanky into a handball between my fingers.

"I have everything Thea and I will need with us," Freddy went on, "so if something should happen, that is to say, if we are stopped, we should be all right. And I will give all the information about you to the chauffeur of the car."

I stared at him.

"What do you mean you will be leaving, Freddy? Will you leave me alone in the car? Where are you going, and why can't I go with you?"

The questions swirled and I was frightened. Freddy knelt down next to me and put his arms about me.

"Little Thing, remember that Thea's friends were very likely killed when Rotterdam was bombed? Well, Thea wants to go there, and rightly so, and find out whatever she can about them. She wants to make sure that they are not still alive and in need of help."

I returned the hanky to Freddy – a misshapen ball – even as I begged. "Can't I come with you? And maybe you should both put on the green uniforms again, Freddy."

"No, and no. No, you can't come along, and no, I don't believe the uniforms will be necessary any longer, Linnet. There are other persons who will need them more than we do."

I could not process all the information Freddy was giving me. Thea stood off to the side and contemplated us. She was fighting tears. I could see her face move in a funny way and her chin was wobbling. Jeroen, who had stationed himself close to the road, now called out.

"Car coming, folks. Get ready to get on board quickly. The driver will be in a hurry."

Thea picked up the suitcase. Freddy, as well, suddenly had a bag in his hand. I recognized it. It was the bag which Thea promised I might use should I ever go for a visit sometime. And now I didn't want to visit. I just wanted to go home.

"Are you ready, Little Thing?"

I did not answer but followed Freddy up the slope towards the road. My legs were wooden. Thea made up the rear.

The car was dark–blue and quite square. As a matter of fact, it was boxy–looking. On any given day, I would have been beside my-self with joy to be given such a new experience as driving in a car. But at this point, I could not focus. The refrain that kept repeating itself in my head was *"Freddy and Thea are leaving me. Soon I will be all alone.*" Jeroen held the front door of the car open. Then he bent over and pulled the front seat forward so that an opening was created through which a passenger could step into the rear of the car. Freddy waved Thea inside and motioned that I should climb in and sit next to her in the back seat. Then he followed, sitting down on my left. A man was stationed behind the steering wheel, a wheel which somewhat resembled the wheel in the boat. Though it had no spokes, it was brown and shiny. The man, who wore a brown overcoat, turned his head towards us when we were settled, offered a warm smile.

"Hello," he said, and we responded by saying "Hello" back to him.

"My name is Karel," he went on, still smiling, "Freddy knows me, of course, because we've been friends for a long time, but you two ladies don't. Just make yourselves as comfortable as you can in the back there, and we'll be off."

Then he turned frontward again, motioning to Jeroen to shut the door. But how could I be comfortable with the knowledge inside me that Freddy and Thea would be going away from me soon?

"Have a good trip," Jeroen called out as he slammed the door shut. And the car began its journey, began its journey away from the island and also, in a sense, away from Freddy and Thea.

"Freddy," I began, after we had been on the road for a few minutes, "Freddy, when is it that will you be leaving me?"

Thea, who had been sitting motionless the whole time, put her right arm around me. "Oh, Linnet," she whispered, "I wish there were some other way, but I really have to go to Rotterdam. I have to find out if my friends are still alive."

"I know," I whispered back, "because if I thought that something had happened to you, I would go and see if you were still alive. It's just . . . it's just that I've never been alone before. Except, I guess, just before you found me. You know when I was in the wooden box. Then I was alone too, wasn't I?"

Freddy coughed. He began a sentence, but didn't finish, and his words didn't make a lot of sense. I remembered that Freddy had been gone from the cottage in the past, sometimes for as long as a week. Because he knew so much about birds, he was sometimes asked to give speeches about them at conferences, and then he had to travel away from us. Those were the days that Thea and I had been alone, without Freddy, but we had been together. She had made pancakes for breakfast and buckwheat with sugar and butter for lunch. And then Freddy would come back and we would celebrate and have a special meal with flowers on the table and a special fruit drink to go with our food. But to be alone with both Freddy and Thea gone, that had never, ever happened to me before.

"Linnet," Thea began again, "Little Thing, we will be back. And Karel will bring you to a place where some people are waiting for you."

"What people?"

"Well, they are Freddy's relatives. They . . . ." She stopped rather helplessly and looked at Freddy.

"You tell her about them, Freddy."

Freddy lay his large hand overtop of mine. "Well, Linnet, the people you will be staying with are my father and my stepmother."

"Why did they never come to visit us on the island?" It was the first thing that came to my mind. Somehow the fact that they had never come to see us seemed unfriendly on their part.

"Well, you see," Freddy squirmed a bit next to me, hunting for words, "Well, you see, my father owns a bakery."

"A bakery?"

Instantly I visualized the bakery on the island. I loved going there. The smells were so good and the lady there was always so very kind even though she did talk a lot. Sometimes she gave me a cookie, sometimes a chocolate, and sometimes a slice of warm bread.

"Yes, a bakery."

"Did your father let you help in the shop when you were little? Did you make cakes, Freddy?"

"Yes, he did and yes, I did make cakes on occasion."

"What is a stepmother?"

"Well, when I was about sixteen years old, my mother died. She had something called the Spanish Influenza."

"What is that, Freddy?"

"Well, Little Thing, Spanish Influenza is an infection. My mother had a fever, a high fever, and she coughed a lot. She had to stay in bed. Many, many people had this influenza and many people died."

I was quiet and stroked his hand, before asking, "Did she die?"

"Yes, she died," Freddy said softly, "and I was not there to say goodbye to her. I was sent away, you see, because my father was afraid that I might catch the influenza and become sick also."

There was a pause and we passed trees, a pond and a park. There were pieces of sky that floated past the car window. Was it the same sky that I had seen on the island?

Freddy went on talking. "Six months after I came back home, my father married my mother's sister, my aunt. Her name was Adri.

So my aunt became my stepmother. A stepmother is someone who marries your father after your mother dies."

"I see."

I didn't really see, but one thing was clear. When Freddy said Adri's name, he was not happy.

"Why did he marry Adri, Freddy?"

"Because he couldn't run the bakery by himself, Little Thing. He had too much work to do."

"Why didn't you help him?"

"Well, I did, but I was set to go away to school, Linnet. I wanted to study zoology and specifically ornithology."

"I'm glad you met Thea, Freddy," I comforted, for Freddy's voice was becoming terse and brusque. It was the voice he took on when he sent in an article to a magazine about birds and it was rejected; it was the voice he had taken on when he told me that there would be bad weather.

"I'm glad he met me too," Thea joined in with a rather sad smile.

"Did you meet Adri and Freddy's father?" I asked her.

"No," Thea answered and then turned her face away from me to look out the window.

"Why not?"

Freddy cleared his throat. "Well, Little Thing, I probably better tell you now, because Adri will familiarize you with what happened sooner or later."

"Tell me about what?" I asked, leaning my head into his side.

"About the fact that my father and Adri don't like Thea."

"Why not?" I answered, mystified, for what was not to like about my Thea?

"Because," Freddy haltingly began, but then Thea leaned over me and put her hand over his mouth, even as she had done with me when I was not supposed to speak.

"Freddy," she said, "it's not wise. Really, it's not wise at this point."

"But they will . . ." he started, but again she stopped him.

"No, they won't."

"You are probably right."

It was quiet again for a moment. I was totally bewildered.

"Linnet," Freddy took up the conversation again, "Little Thing, it is enough for you to know that my father, although perhaps not so much as my stepmother, did not approve of my marriage to Thea. They forbade me to come back home if I married her, and I have never done so. You . . . ." He stopped again, and I was worried. If I were to go and stay with people who did not like my Thea, how could I bear it?

"Can't I come with you?"

It seemed to me that this would solve the problem.

"No, Little Thing. It will be too dangerous."

"Oh."

I bleakly stared at the floorboard of the car. It held a rubber mat – a black mat. Our feet were all on the floor mat, except that mine didn't quite reach. Very soon, Freddy's and Thea's feet would walk where I couldn't follow. I wished I were small enough to crawl into Thea's pocket and so be carried along wherever she went.

"You know, Linnet, if you are ever scared or lonely, there is a person to whom you can go who will be very kind to you."

I looked up into Freddy's face curiously, half-thinking and half-expecting that he would mention God. After all, several people had told me about Him in the last twenty–four hours. But Freddy did not mention God.

"There is a neighbor, a very nice neighbor, who lives right next door to the bakery. She used to be friends with my mother. Her name is Sanne."

"Did you go to her when you were scared, Freddy?"

"Yes, I did."

Karel, the chauffeur, briefly turned his face towards the back.

"We'll be at the railroad station directly, Freddy. I figure it'll take us about five minutes or so before we get there, and I can stop long enough only for you to get your luggage from the boot – not much longer."

"Thanks, Karel."

My heart started thumping. I clutched at both Thea's and Freddy's arms.

"When will you come for me?"

Above my head I knew they were exchanging a look, a look that said it would not be sometime soon. Thea's right arm enfolding my back tightened.

"Will you think of me, Little Thing?"

"You know I will, Thea," I began to cry. "You know that I love you."

"And every night will you hear me say it, Little Thing? Will you hear me say that I love you more than anything?"

"Yes," I sobbed, "of course I will."

Freddy took out his hanky and blew his nose. When he was done, I took it from his hands and blew mine.

"Linnet," he said, "sad birds still sing."

I nodded just as Karel turned around again.

"Get ready to leave," he said. "I can only stay around the station for a very brief period. Do you have everything ready, Freddy?"

Freddy reached into his pocket, checking to see if it held his wallet. "Yes, I do," he said, "and thank you, Karel, for taking Linnet on to my father."

After we had watched Freddy and Thea's figures disappear into the large station building, and Karel had begun to slowly drive away, he turned his face towards me for a moment.

"Why don't you climb out of the backseat, Linnet," he said, patting the place next to himself, "and sit up here in the front seat with me."

Wiping my wet nose with the back of my hand, I clambered over to the front, awkwardly falling down on the seat next to Karel. As I straightened my clothes and sat down properly, he reached into his coat pocket, took out a large white handkerchief similar to Freddy's, and passed it to me.

"Here," he said, "have a good blubber and you'll feel a great deal better."

"Thank you, Karel," I managed through congested nostrils, and blew hard into the cloth.

It did help somewhat and I was able to give him a somewhat lopsided smile.

"That's the spirit, Linnet," he sang out, even as the car speeded up considerably, "and we'll get you settled with Freddy's folks before you know it. I'll make sure they don't eat you, and if I can, I'll even drop by from time to time to make sure you're all right."

I timidly glanced at him from under my eyelashes. Karel was a big man, even siting down behind the steering wheel he was sizable.

A grey cap cockily sat astride his head, and a brown overcoat hugged his broad frame. Feeling my eyes on him, although I tried to be discreet about it, he gave me a sympathetic grin.

"Must be tough for you, Linnet," he tossed over to me in a good–hearted manner, "must be tough to have your folks leave like that. But they're on a good mission, and we all have to do our share."

I gravely agreed by nodding solemnly. His kind words actually gave me the feeling that I was part of Freddy's and Thea's mission, and it was a feeling that bolstered my worth.

"Will it take a long time, Karel," I asked, "to get to Freddy's bakery?"

"Well, now," he pondered, "the roads are fairly empty, except for a few bicycles, so I would think it would take us about one hour. Would you like a licorice to suck away the time?"

It sounded agreeable to me. I had not eaten any breakfast. I rather began to like Karel very much.

"Yes, please."

He took out a roll of licorice candies and handed it to me.

"You can keep it, Linnet," he continued in a conspiratorial tone, "and whenever the gloomies threaten to overcome you, have a licorice and remember that old Karel gave them to you and that he sure thinks you're one brave girl."

"Thank you."

Then, in spite of myself, a tear dropped down onto Karel's white handkerchief, but I wiped it away quickly, hoping that he wouldn't notice. After all, he was trying so hard to encourage me, and seeing me cry again might make him feel unappreciated. The licorice was salted and I did love it so. Sometimes Freddy brought me licorice. Thea didn't approve and said it was bad for my teeth.

"Well, Linnet," Karel said, "and what is it you like to do?"

So I told him about birds, seals and periwinkles, only I said nothing about Jůrgen. Karel was a splendid listener, although he regularly stopped to ask questions. But he had, after all, not grown up on the island. Before I knew it, the inevitable came.

"Here we are, Poppet," Karel suddenly declared. "How time flies when you're being entertained."

We had slowed down and were driving into a village. I had seen its name – Steendorp – on a sign we passed. The main thoroughfare was lined with trees and the road itself was formed of small, round, lump–shaped cobbles that caused the car to thump, thump a bit as it drove. Red–shingled roofs flanked thatched gables on either side of the street. Two- and three–storied homes stood across from one another. A big church could be seen at the end of the main road, its steeple pointing straight up, resembling I thought, an exclamation mark, as if it were saying, "Is this not a fine avenue?!" and "Am I not a great church?"

A river drifted, black and velvety, at the back of the houses on my right side, and there were lots of gardens. Karel was driving very slowly. I saw a woman pushing a baby carriage right between several children playing hopscotch on the sidewalk. Ahead of us, a middle-aged man peddled his bicycle on the cobblestones heading towards the church.

"Do you know where the bakery is, Karel?" I asked, my voice suddenly small.

"Well, and do ducks know how to fly?" he responded, and in spite of myself I had to grin.

It had long ago stopped drizzling, and a fine, blue sky overarched the village. Karel turned the steering wheel to the left. Slowly the car turned onto a secondary lane. Much smaller than the main road, several lamp posts rose from the sidewalk. Ten seconds or so into the lane gave me my first view of the bakery. Its facade was old, and the second story had a nine–paned window held in place by black glazing. Beneath that window hung a brown, wooden panel. On the panel large letters painted green spelled out *Bread, Cake, and Pastry*. Driving closer, more words on the main floor bakery window became visible.

"Veerman's Bakery." They were white letters and were printed boldly. I read all the words presented in the thick lettering in a dilatory fashion, as if reading them in that way would cause delay, would stop the inevitable moment when I would have to leave the car.

"You read well, Poppet," Karel commented admiringly, even as he edged the car close to the sidewalk in front of the store.

"Freddy and Thea taught me."

"Well, then," he went on, "won't the folks here be proud of you. I only learned to read when I was about twice your age."

He turned off the motor before reaching over and taking my hand. "Now remember, Poppet," he said softly, "you are a soldier and doing your assigned job. Let me see a smile and do Freddy and Thea credit. Chin up, shoulders back, and let's face the biscuit makers together."

I managed all of half a smile. Karel opened his door, edged his heavy bulk out, and stood on the road. Then he strode over to the sidewalk, reached my door and opened it as well. While I climbed out, he took my bag from the boot of the car and brought it over.

"Your luggage, Madam," he said.

"Will you take me to the door, Karel?"

"Of course, Poppet," he answered as he took my hand. "Karel won't leave until you're settled."

8

Before either Karel or myself had reached the entryway of the bakery, we heard the copper doorbell attached to the door ring. It was a lovely, friendly sound and I instantly loved it. A silver-haired gentleman, short and slender, stood revealed in the portal even as the sound died away. He did not look like Freddy in the least. Somehow, I had expected a tall and robust sort of man, a muscular man wearing a white apron, sporting a dab of flour on both his cheeks, and wearing a white, tall baker's hat. But although the man was wearing an apron, he did not at all make me think of my Freddy. Absorbed by his appearance, I stopped dead in my tracks. Perhaps this was the wrong place; perhaps this was after all, a mistake. And that was fine by me. I tightened my grip on Karel's hand, and he pressed back gently, reassuringly.

"Hello," he greeted the man jovially. "Do I have the honor of meeting Freddy Veerman's father?"

The trim man, who had fixed a rather intense gaze on me, smiled a slow smile, revealing a set of fine, white teeth, except that the right front one was slightly chipped.

"Yes, you do."

It was a thin voice and carried little inflection. I wondered if Mr. Veerman knew how to sing or recite a poem.

"Well then," Karel went on, "my name is Karel Haansma, and I have the pleasure of introducing you to your granddaughter, Linnet Veerman."

"How do you do," Mr. Veerman said, continuing to focus his attention on me. His eyes were green, not blue as Freddy's were, and not as open. There was a lidded secretiveness about them, as if he were hiding something. He went on, his voice bland.

"I see that my son did not come to bring you himself."

"That is," I heard myself answer immediately and a little shrilly, "because you do not want Thea to come to your house."

Karel squeezed my hand again. This time the squeeze was not reassuring but warning. Mr. Veerman stopped fixating on me. His stare descended to the sidewalk. His voice, when he responded, had turned defensive.

"You are addressing your grandfather, Child," he said, "and in my day, we were taught to speak with respect to our elders."

"I'm sorry, Sir," I returned, hearing Thea admonish me in my heart. "It is just that I love Thea and . . . ."

"Do you speak of your *Mem* as Thea?" he interrupted.

"Yes," I answered, for had she not found me in the box and did that not make her my *Mem* and my Thea both.

"I see."

Karel took several steps forward towards Mr. Veerman, pulling me along. A cadre of German soldiers had just turned the corner of the street into the lane. They wore the same gray-green uniforms that Freddy and Thea had shed earlier that morning. Mr. Veerman didn't know that Freddy and Thea had worn those uniforms. The soldiers were marching towards us, and Mr. Veerman began to motion rapidly with his arms that we should move on and come into the shop. There was no help for it. The bakery would be my home. The lovely-sounding jingle vibrated through the air again when the door closed behind us after we passed over the threshold. The chime piqued up my curiosity, and I wondered if Freddy had also listened to it.

"Did Freddy like the bell?"

The words slipped out of my mouth before I thought. A woman, a rather heavy–set woman, was standing behind the bakery counter. The wall behind her was covered with square white and blue tiles. If Mr. Veerman was thin, weighing less than a pail-full of sand, this lady had a generous measure of flesh and surely weighed more than a grey seal. She was studying me even as Mr. Veerman had studied me. I gave her a wide smile just to show I had not meant to be offensive by asking about Freddy and the bell, and she reciprocated by giving me a thin pursing of the lips, which produced two small dimples in her plump cheeks. But her eyes, her gray eyes, did not twinkle along with those cheeks.

"If he thought it had wings and flew, then he probably did like them. The truth is that Freddy never told us."

It was Mr. Veerman who answered.

"Well, I must say," Karel interjected, "that it smells delicious in here. There's no aroma like that of freshly baked bread. My nose is in heaven, and that is a fact."

Ignoring his words, Mr. Veerman walked over and stood directly in front of me. "Well, Child," he said, and his voice was neither friendly nor unfriendly, "do you think you might call me *Pake*?"

"*Pake*?"

Pake was the word for "grandfather," and Karel, who was still holding my hand, compressed it again. It meant, *"Say yes."*

"Yes," I answered, and my voice was a little squeaky.

Would Freddy mind if I called his father *Pake*?

"Very well," Mr. Veerman rejoined, rubbing his hands together in a satisfied sort of way – a way that instantly made me think of Freddy. "That's fine then."

He glanced over at the counter, after which he stood quietly for a moment before interrogating me again. "And do you think, Linnet, that you might also call this lady here, this lady who is my wife, *Tante* Adri?"

I looked down at my shoes. This was a very different question. *Tante* Adri did not like Thea and Freddy and Thea had not wanted to tell me why that was. Karel squeezed my hand in a hardy fashion suggesting a positive answer. Since my shoes were not injecting any alternative answers into either my feet or my brain, I wavered and stared up at Karel with doubtful eyes. He smiled down at me.

"Sure, Poppet," he whispered, "it will be fine to call this lady *Tante* Adri. There is, after all, as Shakespeare said, nothing in a name."

I shifted my gaze back to Mr. Veerman, my new *pake*. "Yes, *Pake*, I think I can do that."

Karel let go of my hand and clapped me on the back with his left hand. His right hand set down my bag in front of the glass counter. He set it down so hard that all the cookies displayed within the counter shook. *Tante* Adri frowned. But Karel took no notice.

"Well, that's it then," he posited, "I suggest, Mr. Veerman, that you give this child a good lunch. She's had nothing to eat all day, and I would assume that she is famished."

Mr. Veerman rubbed his hands together again.

"Certainly," he said, "certainly we will feed this child. And you, Mr. Haansma, can we also offer you a bite to eat?"

"You know," Karel said, "ordinarily I would jump at the chance of dining at a bakery, especially one which offers so many delightful delicacies as I see here in front of me. But the truth is that I have other pressing errands to run yet today."

A hard lump came up in my throat, and I swallowed. It would not do to cry on first acquaintance. It would not do at all. Karel knelt down and enfolded me in a bear hug.

"Chin up, Poppet," he said softly, "and remember, I'll try to be by from time to time to see how you're keeping."

"I know," I whispered back, "I know. I love you, Karel."

After Karel had exited through the bakery door, and the lovely sound of the bell had faded, *Tante* Adri came out from behind the counter. To the left of that counter I could see that the bakery extended into a room that held an oven as well as a large wooden table. The table was sprinkled white with flour.

"Well, now, Linnet," *Tante* Adri said, as she made her way towards me with short but purposeful steps, repeating, "Well, now Linnet, let me show you where you will sleep so that you can unpack your suitcase before we have some lunch."

Like *Pake*, *Tante* Adri was covered with a white apron, only hers was considerably wider than his. A blue cap, a cap which was just a bit crooked, was set on her straight, browning hair. The color of the cap perfectly matched the tiles behind Tante Adri's head. Picking up my bag, she walked out through an exit to the right of the counter. I followed her, and hardly believed it when *Pake* smiled at me as I passed him.

"See you later, Granddaughter," he whispered, and I couldn't help but feel a trifle better about having come and about having agreed to call him *Pake*.

The door *Tante* Adri had taken led to a small hall with a stairway on its left. "Up we go," she directed, and up she went, her blue cap bobbing.

It was a rather steep flight of steps, and I counted fifteen steps altogether. It was definitely not as high as the ladder in the Fire Tower on the island, but longer than the stairs in our cottage. *Tante* Adri's broad frame proceeded at quite a pace. The stairs were wooden and well-worn, but they seemed to bear our weight well. The eighth step, however, creaked with an unhealthy whine as we ascended. *Don't go up. Don't go up.* But I had no choice.

"Here we are then," *Tante* Adri puffed as she reached the top, "and now to the left. Just follow me."

I did follow her even as my mind fleetingly registered that this second hallway held three doors, two of them open. These two were bedrooms, and what the third room held was a mystery. But neither of the bedrooms was apparently to be mine, because we continued up a second stairway.

"Up we go," repeated *Tante* Adri, and up she went.

This second set of steps was just as steep as the first had been. But because this flight curved sharply to the right, it seemed more difficult and more arduous to climb. Consequently, I was amazed at the rapidity at which Tante Adri was ascending.

"Are you following me, Linnet?"

"Yes, *Tante* Adri."

The wallpaper next to these stairs was covered with faded roses. The roses were without odor, without thorns, and without life. They drooped sadly next to the steps. Perhaps I should tell *Tante* Adri they needed water, but somehow I doubted that she would smile as Thea would have done.

"Here we are then." *Tante* Adri had reached the top step and progressed through a stairwell onto the flooring of what appeared to me to be a loft, or attic. "*Pake* and I thought this might be a cozy, little bedroom for you. What do you think?"

She conveyed the information with her back towards me. Setting the bag on the floor, and after pulling on a light switch chain dangling from the ceiling, she advanced slowly toward a high-backed chair in front of a small cot. She was now breathing rather heavily. Turning as she sat down, expectantly awaiting a response to her question, she sighed, simultaneously taking out a handkerchief from her white apron pocket to wipe a glistening forehead.

Still standing on the top step, I now stepped onto the wooden planks of attic flooring. It was obvious that this bedroom space was directly under the sloped roof of the bakery. Slanted timber beams ran down from a V–shaped ceiling. A strong smell of dust mingled with mold enveloped me, and I saw a small mouse scamper under the bed. *Tante* Adri coughed, still awaiting a comment. She had not seen the mouse, and I suspected she would not be pleased if I were to mention the little animal. Having had Belle, we had few, if any, mice in the cottage.

"What do you think?" *Tante* Adri repeated, resting her hands in her lap.

There was a little door towards the right side. It was perhaps hiding a closet. There was a window to the left side – a small, round window covered with cobwebs and dust. Encased in the brick outside wall, it was rather filthy. Thea would not have stood for the dirt or the dust around it, but Thea was not here.

"I very much like the window," I responded, because, in spite of the grime, I did.

"The window?" *Tante* Adri's response was somewhat perplexed. She followed my gaze towards the dusty glass pane and I reiterated.

"Yes, I always love looking out windows." I remembered the dunes then and the fine, wide island sky, and a hard lump grew in my stomach. *Chin up, Poppet.* Karel's voice resounded in my head. It made me straighten my back. I focused on the cot. It held a blue bedspread, a crocheted bedspread.

"Blue is a good color for a bedspread," I went on. "It will remind me of the sky when I'm going to sleep." Again *Tante* Adri appeared somewhat baffled.

"Well, that's your affair, I suppose. You're free to think what you like before you go to sleep. Now tell me if you think this dresser behind me will do for your clothes."

I had not noted it, but there it stood behind *Tante* Adri. It was a dismal and drab–looking dresser with four horizontal drawers stacked one above the other. Wooden knobs protruded from the centre of each section. I supposed that all my belongings would easily fit into it. "It is very curious," I said, for indeed it was.

Tante Adri sighed. "You are the curious one, Child. Well, I'll leave you to unpack, and after you unpack, you may come down for a bite to eat."

"Thank you, *Tante* Adri."

Slowly she rose, had another good look at me, and with small but quick steps, strode heavily back to the stair opening. I watched her go down and worried that she might not be able to descend as easily as she had ascended. But there was no problem.

When she was gone, I sat down on the cot. *Tante* Adri did not seem all bad now that I had seen her. Why did she not like Thea? Would she like me? Did it matter? *"Linnet, not so many questions."* I could literally feel Thea's hand cover my mouth. Walking over to the round window, I wished that *Tante* Adri would have left her hand-kerchief behind, because then I could have cleaned the window.

Little sounds scurrying across the planks made me turn my head back towards the cot, just in time to see the mouse skittering behind the dresser. Well, in any case, I would have a friend here. It was not a bird, but perhaps a mouse would do. Maybe I could teach it tricks. Turning my head back to the window, I rubbed a small section of it with the cuff of my sleeve. The hazy film partially disappeared, and soft afternoon sunlight exposed finely powdered dust particles floating in the air. A rusty latch lay at the bottom of the pane. It was very much like the latch that had been on our privy at the cottage. I tried to slide the corroding, little bolt in effort to open the window, but although it moved a little, it was very stiff. Perhaps later I could clean and polish it and see if I could get it to budge. My stomach rumbled with hunger, and I yawned at the same time. But I couldn't go down to eat until I emptied the bag.

The floor squeaked a little as I tiptoed towards my bag. I don't know why I tiptoed. Perhaps because I wanted to retain a feeling of privacy. There was neither a door to this attic nor a curtain around my cot. I tipped the bag onto the blue bedspread. The first thing I noted falling out of the bag onto the bedspread was a picture. Not a drawn picture of an animal, such as Thea was wont to make for me, but a photograph. I lifted it up and looked into the smiling faces of Freddy and Thea. They were standing next to one another, arms draped around one another's shoulders, and at the bottom Thea had written, "*Hello, Little Thing. We love you.*"

"Hello, I love you too," I whispered and held their likenesses next to my heart so that I would be in the photograph too, and then took it away and looked at it again.

I placed the portrait on the dresser, and as I put away socks, undershirts, undies, and nightgown into the bottom drawer, I kept taking quick peeks up to make sure Freddy and Thea were still smiling at me. My special knitted white sweater with the zipper on the shoulder, and the blue knitted jumper with the rainbow lines splashed across its skirt, I gave a special place in the top drawer. Blouses, skirts, and my puffed pants went into the second drawer, and the pencils, paper and bird books went into the remaining drawer.

I took off my coat and hung it on a nail under the window. It was a good spot. My coat was light blue and it added a touch of colour to the rather cheerless interior of the attic. Then I remembered the licorice roll in its pocket and took it out to hide it between the undies in the first drawer. The swinging light bulb in the centre of the room had a long metal chain attached to it. *Tante* Adri had pulled on it to make the bulb shine. Like the window, it was rather drab. I wished that I had a little rug to lay in front of the cot. That might make things a little cosier. Maybe I could ask *Tante* Adri for one.

I turned off the light switch and proceeded down the stairs. When I got to the second landing, I heard the sound of a bird come from one of the rooms. Hesitantly, I stopped and walked down the hall corridor to the now closed doors, stopping by the one from which the sound was emanating. Not able to help myself, I slowly pushed down the door handle and nudged the door open. Peeking my head around the corner, the first thing I perceived was a double poster bed. A parakeet cage stood next to the bed and in front of a window. It was a round metal cage and it hung from a hook on the ceiling. In the cage was a beautiful light–green parakeet sitting on a little swing and chirping.

"Are you looking for something, Linnet?" *Tante* Adri's voice behind me startled me into banging the door shut.

"Uh," I stuttered, "I was . . . I was trying to find the . . . ."

"I see," she replied, suddenly seeming to understand. "The W.C. is across from this door."

She moved to open a brown door across the hall. It was the door that had been closed on our way up. Tinier than a closet, I could see a toilet in it. She beckoned me over and pulled a string attached to the ceiling. It turned on yet another light bulb.

"You sit down," she explained kindly, as if I were a little child, "and when you are done with your job, you pull the chain on the left side of the toilet and it will flush."

I nodded, half–embarrassed and half–relieved.

"You can wash your hands at the sink afterwards, and there's a towel for drying your hands hanging from the rack under the sink."

I nodded again.

"Thank you, *Tante* Adri." As I spoke, I wondered if I would ever be able to get in to see the little parakeet.

"Well, do you want to go to the W.C. before we eat or not?"

Slowly I walked past *Tante* Adri and entered the W.C., closing the door behind me. It was not like our outhouse in the least. We had gotten to our outhouse by walking on the little stone path leading from the backdoor to its wooden door. That wooden door had a good-sized star carved at the top panel – for the smell, Thea had explained. The green-shingled roof of the outhouse sloped down so that the rain would drain off. And its seat was made of wooden slats with a round hole to sit on. Freddy sometimes sprinkled ashes through the hole – that was also for the smell, he said.

Thea would get a bucket of water each day and flush down the waste. We had hung a picture of an eagle on the wall. There was also a picture of the Queen next to the eagle. We talked about whether or not this was respectful, but Freddy said that there could never be too many pictures of the Queen and that since we also had a photograph of her in the kitchen, there was no problem. Our toilet paper consisted of magazine pages cut into squares. Thea had punctured the papers with a needle and thread and had hung them up from the ceiling. They hung at just the right height so that we could reach them when we were sitting on the seat.

At night, when it was too dark for me to find my way to the privy, I was allowed to use a potty tucked away under my cot. Would *Tante* Adri put a potty under my cot? Had she done it? I had not looked. I pulled the chain and the toilet flushed. There was a calendar, a birthday calendar, hanging on the tiny wall behind the toilet.

The New Has Come

"Are you done, Linnet?" *Tante* Adri was waiting for me. It made me uncomfortable. I washed my hands and dried them on a little, yellow towel. Then I opened the door and stepped back into the corridor.

"There you are," *Tante* Adri did truly smile this time, and her dimples came out again, "so now we'll go directly down and have some sandwiches."

I could hear the parakeet chirping in the bedroom. He must be lonely.

Tante Adri led the way down the stairs. Upon reaching the bottom, she turned left and made her way straight through a small corridor. Following closely behind, I found myself in a kitchen/dining room of sorts. It held a table covered with a red checkered tablecloth, three white plates, cream enamel mugs, a butter dish, a Delfts-blue milk jug, and a basket of white bread. I digested the scene in a glance, my stomach making little, gurgling noises.

"Sit down, Child," *Tante* Adri said. "I'll go call your *Pake*."

The table faced a window. I sat down in the chair opposite it so that I could look out at the backyard. White, lace curtains hung across the panes, and three geraniums graced the sill. It prevented me from seeing too much of the outside. I was very tired and had an inane hankering to lay my head on top of my plant and go to sleep. The smell of the bread kept me awake. It smelled so fresh and looked so crusty and appetizing. To my disappointment, however, there was no cheese in sight, just a jar of jam.

"Here we are."

Tante Adri, followed by *Pake,* walked in. Making a beeline for the table, they both sat down. I was hungry, and when they were seated, reached for the bread basket.

""Watch your manners, Child," *Tante* Adri's admonition rang out and my hand shot back. "Be served, and don't serve yourself first! Fold your napkin on your lap. And we haven't even prayed yet."

"Prayed?"

"Yes. Didn't you pray where you come from?"

Four eyes fixed on me, and I understood from the tone of the question that praying was terribly important. "Yes," I lied, thinking to protect both Freddy and Thea. "I just forgot."

"Well, fold your hands and close your eyes." I was happy with the instruction and did as I was told.

Pake's dry voice began: "Our great God and heavenly Father."

I peeked. Was God in this house too? Willem had said with great conviction that He was everywhere. Was He in this room and perhaps sitting at this table? But I could see no one, no one at all besides *Tante* Adri and *Pake*. At this point *Tante* Adri opened her eyes, and these eyes sternly monitored me. I quickly squeezed my lids shut.

"We invoke Your blessing on this food and drink. We thank You for it. Amen."

There was quiet now. I was half afraid to open my eyes, but because of the stillness, presumed *Pake* was done with his praying.

"Would you like a piece of bread now, Linnet?"

"Yes, please."

"You are allowed two pieces, Linnet. One with jam and one with contentment."

"Contentment?"

"That means," *Tante* Adri explained, "a piece of bread with just butter."

"Oh."

She reached for my plate, buttered a piece of bread, and spread some jam on it. Then she placed another next to it and proceeded to butter that as well. Cutting up both slices into small squares, she positioned the assortment in front of me. My enamel cup was then filled with milk and I was ready to go.

"Use your fork, Linnet."

We had never used forks on the island to eat our bread. But I was willing to do anything at this point as I was starving.

"How is Freddy?" It was *Pake* who spoke, his hands busy buttering his bread, and his eyes down on his plate. What could I say?

"He is fine, *Pake*."

That sentence was safe. It held no disturbing message. Had Freddy sat here once and had he prayed, or listened to a prayer such as *Pake* had prayed just now? Freddy had never once told me about prayer or about God. I chewed as I reflected and stared at the geraniums. They were red, just like Thea's. I wondered what would happen to her geraniums. They had stood in the window sill when we left, had stood like red soldiers. Without water, they would die. Perhaps the Germans would check our cottage and they would water . . . .

"Linnet, don't day-dream. *Pake* is talking to you."

I sat up straight and turned by eyes to *Pake*.

"I asked," his dreary voice addressed me, "if you went to school."

"No, *Pake*," I answered. "I'm just five, but I know how to read and write. I can add and subtract a little too, because Thea . . . ," here I stopped abruptly, because I wasn't sure if the word "Thea" was permitted at this table or in this house.

But there were no reprisals, no angry sounds, so I kept going. "Well, Thea taught me a bit every day. I know many birds also. Freddy taught me about birds and their names."

I took another bite. It was fresh, crusty bread, and the jam, although spread thinly, was good too.

"Well," *Pake* responded, following it up with another, "Well."

I kept eating even as *Tante* Adri, shifting her bulk around on her chair, took over for *Pake*. "You know about birds you say? Well, we have a bird – a parakeet – in our bedroom."

"*Melopsittacus undulatus*," I automatically responded, my mouth half full of two squares of bread of contentment. "That s the species for parakeet."

Tante Adri stopped eating and gave *Pake* a look even as she lifted her eyebrows – a look that said, "*I think the child is showing off*" and I suppose that I was.

"Do you know anything about cleaning the kitchen or dusting shelves and sweeping floors?" she asked me next.

I shook my head. "Not much, *Tante* Adri," I confessed, "but I know how to make my bed and set the table."

I could graphically see our cosy cottage kitchen, and I remembered how I had set plates down on our tablecloth, plates with a daisy pattern on them. What had happened to those dishes? Had Freddy been able to take them away so that the Germans wouldn't steal them?

"Do you know how to sew, Child?" *Tante* Adri went on.

I shook my head again. I hated sewing with a fierce passion. My hands always became sweaty and uncoordinated when Thea tried to teach me how to embroider or knit. Thea herself, though, was very gifted and could sew anything to which she put her hand.

But *Tante* Adri wouldn't want to know that. *Tante* Adri didn't like Thea. Why not?

"Perhaps," *Pake* said, "we could send Linnet for sewing lessons at Sanne's."

Sanne? My ears perked up. Freddy had mentioned Sanne this very morning. *You know, Linnet, if you are ever scared, or lonely, there is a person to whom you can go who will be very kind to you.*

"I could teach her myself," *Tante* Adri proposed, immediately making me very worried, "but it is true that the shop keeps me more than busy. Linnet, however, will have to do her share of work around the bakery too, Albert, if she is to go to Sanne."

I didn't know that *Pake's* name was Albert. I yawned. Both *Pake* and Tante Adri responded to the yawn. "Hand in front of your mouth, Linnet," was *Tante* Adri's contribution, and *Pake* added, "What time did you get up this morning, Linnet?"

Pake observed me with something of pity and compassion as he spoke.

"I don't think I got up," I answered, "because I didn't really go to bed."

My plate was empty now and suddenly increasingly weariness took hold of my limbs. I sincerely hoped that *Tante* Adri wouldn't want me to sweep and dust after this meal.

"I think that she should go to bed," *Pake* proffered, and to my delight, Tante Adri agreed with a nod of her head.

"But first," she said, "we should read the Bible."

Again my ears became attuned. *Tante* Adri got up, walked over to a sideboard next to the kitchen sink, and picked up a large book from one of its shelves. It was a larger book than any of the volumes we'd had in the cottage on our bookshelf under the stairs. *Tante* Adri set the brown book on the table in front of *Pake*, who reached into his vest pocket and took out a pair of glasses.

"Where are you in your Bible reading?" he demanded to know, even as he put on the spectacles.

"I forgot." My answer came quickly. An inherent feeling kicked in that somehow there were many things that I did not know, things about which Thea and Freddy had not told me. Were they bad things? Should I know of them? *Pake* paged through the book and I yawned again. My eyes wanted to close, and I was progressively flagging in consistent thinking.

"What story would you like?" *Pake* asked as he peered at me overtop of his glasses. "It's your first day here, so I will let you choose."

It was a tricky question, and I was so sleepy.

"Well, *Pake*," I replied, smothering another yawn, "I think I would like the very first one."

"You mean creation?" he said.

"Yes."

Pake began to read. He had a thin voice and a rather soft one. I tried very hard to listen.

"In the beginning, God created the heavens and the earth."

I was pleased that God was mentioned. It must be the right Bible then that *Pake* was reading, the Bible that Jürgen had told me to read about God.

"And the earth was without form, and void; and darkness was upon the face of the deep. And the Spirit of God moved upon the face of the waters."

No form, void, darkness, face of the deep – these were all words, phrases that did not make sense to me. I rested my head against the back of the chair and closed my eyes for just a moment. Maybe Tante Adri would think that I was praying.

"And God said, Let there be light: and there was light."

I opened my eyes again.

"And God saw the light, that it was good: and God divided the light from the darkness."

I had divided shells into piles of large shells and small shells, and I had divided the *speculaas* cookies just the other day when I had served tea to Freddy and Thea. Six cookies I had divided into two each: two for Thea, two for Freddy, and two for me. But I had never divided light from darkness. How would you do that? I yawned again.

"And God called the light Day, and the darkness He called Night. And the evening and the morning were the first day."

At this moment, I suddenly fell off my chair, and both *Tante* Adri and *Pake* stood over me.

"I think that she should go to bed," *Pake* said, even as he put an arm under my shoulders. I was surprised by the strength in his small frame. He was not big like Freddy, but he was strong. And that was the last thing I remembered until the next morning.

9

It became a daily routine for me to sweep the kitchen/dining room floor after breakfast, after which I was instructed to go on to sweep the bakery shop, which included the room with the oven and the wooden table. There was lots of dust there, white dust. I didn't mind these tasks at all. When they were done, I also had to make sure that the shop door (both inside and outside) was clean. *Tante* Adri showed me how to fill a small pail with soapy water, and supplied me with a host of rags.

Carrying the pail, usually swaying as I went, I would make my way into the shop. It was warm there and smelled wonderful. Then, going down on my hands and knees, I sopped a rag and scrubbed until the floor by the door, as well as the door and its handle, were shiny and wet. Another rag cloth served to dry off the suds. *Tante* Adri had demonstrated and appeared to be pleased with the result. At least she never scolded me for doing it wrong.

Washing the door was a little like washing the pump handle, which had been one of my chores at the cottage. I especially liked cleaning the outside of the bakery door as this gave me a chance to say "hello" to people passing on the street. Sometimes customers would stop and study the wares displayed in the shop windows, and I might say: *"The bread is very tasty today"* or *"The pastry is yummy. I can tell you that because I had a bite."* Generally, most passers-by would chuckle, and often they would come into the store. One lady even told *Pake* that I was a super salesgirl and an asset to his establishment.

After these chores were done, my mid-morning task was to write out a chapter of the Bible in a notebook as I sat at the kitchen table. This took a considerable amount of time, as my printing was much slower and more laborious than my reading. After I finished writing out the chapter, I had to read it out loud, first to myself and then to *Pake* and *Tante* Adri at lunch time. They were continually amazed at my ability to read, but never took the time to ask if I understood what I was reading. And I was too proud to ask for help. The writing assignment began at chapter one of Genesis, the chapter that *Pake* had read that first night I came.

My first Saturday at the bakery led to my introduction of Saturday rules.

"We don't work on Sunday, Linnet," *Tante* Adri told me. "All the chores that we are able to do on Saturday, we perform beforehand."

Little meatballs had to be rolled from a package of hamburger from the butcher's shop for the Sunday soup. *Tante* Adri rolled the first balls, turning pieces of raw meat over and over in her palms until they became small, red orbs. When I surreptitiously tried to taste one, she slapped my hand.

"It'll give you worms," she exclaimed.

Then she carefully watched me wash my hands before letting me attempt to make some. I rather liked doing it. *Tante* Adri also showed me how to scrape and scrub the carrots, as well as cut up onions, both of which were added to the soup. While it was boiling away, she also showed me how to rake the grass in the backyard and how to take in the laundry hanging on the clothesline.

Late Saturday afternoon, I was instructed to sweep the side-walk in front of the shop, so that it would be clean on Sunday morning. *Tante* Adri also demonstrated how to polish *Pake's* black shoes, the shoes that he wore on Sunday.

"We must look our best on Sunday, Linnet."

After I had finished the late Saturday afternoon sweeping and the shoe polishing, *Tante* Adri carried an old, round tin tub from the shed in the back garden into the kitchen. Pail after hot pail of water was deposited into this tub. Then I was unceremoniously told to take off my clothes and to wash myself thoroughly.

At the cottage, we'd had a similar tub, so I was not unfamiliar with how to get in and hunch up my knees. *Pake* had been shooed away, my nightshirt was lying on a nearby kitchen chair, and a piece of sunlight soap was handed to me.

"Wash behind your ears, Linnet. And make sure you scrub your feet."

In spite of myself, I found it cosy to sit in the warm water. And if I closed my eyes, I could almost imagine that I was in the cottage and that Thea was telling me all these things. Afterwards, *Tante* Adri rubbed me dry with a big towel, rubbed me so hard I almost disappeared. As I donned my nightgown, she emptied the tub water into the backyard, after which she called *Pake* for supper. We had pancakes with syrup. Afterwards, stuffed and satisfied, I was hurried up to bed.

The first Sunday morning that I walked to church with *Tante* Adri and *Pake*, I strolled between the two. After waking up, I had put on my special white pullover with the zipper on its shoulder. Overtop of that I had donned the pretty blue jumper that Thea had knit for me last year. It was the most beautiful outfit that I owned, and I always felt like a princess when I wore it. *Tante* Adri clucked approvingly when I came downstairs. I was not ready to tell her that Thea made most of my clothes. Wearing my jumper prompted the feeling within me that Thea would go with me to church and would have her arms wrapped around me when I ventured out to this new place. Jûrgen had told me to go to church so that I could read the Bible. Of course, *Pake* read the Bible every day after supper, but I didn't quite follow what he read. Part of it was that he mumbled and that he spoke so very softly; and part of it was that I did not want to appear ignorant to either him or *Tante* Adri by asking questions.

On the way to church I was instructed several times by both *Pake* and *Tante* Adri that I was not to speak out loud, that I could only whisper, and that under no circumstances could I ask to go to the bathroom. Turning left onto the large, cobblestone street that formed a tee at the end of our lane, we proceeded to trek upwards towards the church. We passed quite a few houses, and they all had lace curtains. I could distinguish no faces behind any of the curtains. It was very quiet outside, although I could hear birds twittering in the trees by the side of the road.

A few people strolled in front of us. *Pake* walked sedately, obviously not in a hurry, not at all like Freddy, who was forever telling me to move faster. This was the road I had traveled on when I first came into town with Karel. I wondered if Karel was going to church too. I wondered if he would come to visit and tell me where Freddy and Thea were.

"Don't drag your feet, Linnet. Lift them up, Child." *Tante* Adri poked a thick finger into my shoulder. I could clearly see the church now with its exclamation steeple at the end of the street. It was a very high steeple. There was a lovely window below its steeple. Round like Karel's steering wheel, it also had spokes like the steering wheel in the boat. Only these were black, glazed spokes, and they made the window seem more like a flower, a rose-colored flower, than a steering wheel.

"Linnet, watch where you are going. Look straight ahead, Child!" *Tante* Adri's voice was soft but sharp.

"Yes, *Tante* Adri."

I brought my tilted neck back down. My blue skirt swished about my knees. *Never mind, Linnet,* Thea said. *Never mind. I will come to church with you. And I will come and get you soon.* But even as I heard the words inside my head, I rather doubted whether she would.

We were at the church now and entered, not through the big front double doors, but through a small side door which immediately ushered us into the heart of the building. Long benches filled the large room from the back to the front. I had never seen such an enormous room, and there were already lots of people sitting down. Tante Adri pushed me to the left. Advancing in front of her, I felt the curious stares of lots of people as they examined me as we paced along the side wall towards the middle of the room.

There was also a section of seats hanging close to the ceiling. It fascinated me, and I wished we were going to sit there. *Pake* later told me that this was called a balcony. It would be wonderful to perch up there like a bird in a tree and to study all the people below.

Tante Adri propelled me towards the right, and I understood I was to navigate between one of the rows and shuffle along until she told me to sit down. The spot she picked was almost in the centre. Her hands took hold of my shoulders, stopping and pushing me down concurrently. I sat down, whereupon she proceeded to pass me, taking her place on my right. *Pake* sat down on my left.

Positioned on the middle left side of the church, I watched as, bit by bit its entirety filled. Black-suited men and women, the women all wearing hats, slowly and sedately paraded by. It seemed very much as if everyone knew exactly where to sit. *Tante* Adri was also wearing hat – a black hat. Her arms folded squarely in front of her, she was a formidable neighbor, and when I began to dangle my feet which did not quite reach the floor, back and forth, her right arm reached over and she pinched my thigh. *Pake* gave no indication whatsoever that he noticed.

Sometimes families would come in and the mother and the children would sit down, but the father would stay in the aisle with his head bowed. After a considerable pause, he would also sit down with his family. I did not know why.

Music began shortly after we came in. I craned my neck to see where it was coming from, but it earned me another pinch. So I poked *Pake* and asked him where it came from. He bent his head and whispered *orgel* in my ear and discretely pointed to the right wall.

There were a number of pipes lined along that wall. Presumably the sound came from the pipes on the wall, but who would have a mouth big enough to play this organ? A giggle welled up within my throat, but remembering the pinches, I suppressed it. The music was lovely. I had once had a mouth organ, but had lost it in the dunes. Thea had been very angry with me. I did not know that I had ever heard such a resonant sounds before, not even on our radio. At times there was a flute-like quality, and I could hear birds – birds that I had never seen – colorful and bright. They flew about the rafters, dancing, squawking, and even mewing.

After we had sat in our seats for close to half an hour, a door opened next to the *kansel* (*Pake* had whisper-told me that this was what the platform in front of the church was called). Men, dressed in black, filed out and walked to different pews in the church and sat down. One of the men though, before he went to sit down, shook the right hand of a black-robed person who remained standing at the bottom of the stairs. His robe was as black as mine had been the night we left the island. Was he going into hiding? But there were two differences between his robe and the one I had worn. His had a small, white collar, and there was no black veil.

The entire room around me became very hushed now. It was as if the people were all holding their breaths together. Then the man in the black robe began to speak, even as he stood at the bottom of the stairs. He had a satiny, smooth voice, and his voice carried throughout the room.

Our help is in the name of the Lord Who made the heavens and the earth. Grace and peace to you from Him Who is and was and Who is to be,

and from the seven spirits before His throne and from Jesus Christ, the
faithful Witness, the Firstborn of the dead and the Ruler of the kings of the
earth. Amen.

I loved the words and remembered some of them. They tasted
good to my heart and mind. It was as if my insides had been hungry
and I was fed by these words. After he spoke, the man climbed the
stairs.

For much of the service, I sat back and studied the people
around me. When there was singing, I read the words of the song
with *Tante* Adri out of her song book. When there was prayer, *Tante*
Adri would pinch me and whisper, *"Close your eyes, Linnet."*

The black–robed man spoke for a very long time, and some of
what he said I heard and some of what he said flew right over my
head like the seagulls flew over my head when we went for a walk
on the strand by the Wadden Sea. There was a money collection.
Pake had told me about that too. Several men steadily traversed the
aisles with what appeared to be very long poles, poles that had little
velvet bags hanging from their ends. I grinned, for it appeared that
all the men were going fishing and there were no fish in church at
all. One by one, the men passed these little bags through the rows of
people and, as the bags passed, people dropped money into them. I
was fascinated.

When it was the turn of our row, and the bag dangled in front
of me, I slowly dropped the penny *Pake* had given me into the silky
appendage. After I had done that, I sincerely wanted to feel the little,
velvet bag with my hands. Would it be as soft as Belle? My desire
grew and my hands began to have a mind of their own. Even as
Tante Adri was about to put her contribution in, I gently took hold

of the wooden rod, endeavouring to stroke the pouch. The man holding the pole must have thought I was going to spoil things, for he immediately lifted the pouch up in a somewhat haphazard and erratic way. *Tante* Adri, who had just bent over slightly to deposit her money, was bumped on the nose and her hat fell off. It was awkward, but I picked up her hat and brushed it off before placing it on her lap. But I could tell by her face that she was not at all happy. So I leaned back waiting for another pinch, but fortunately *Pake* shook his head at *Tante* Adri, which I took to mean that he thought she should forgive me.

When we came home later, there was a wonderful luncheon of Sunday soup. Seven little meatballs swam in my bowl. Afterwards, *Pake* and *Tante* Adri went to their bedroom for a nap, and I went to my room and took out my bird books. Walking through the attic, I pretended that I was out for a stroll with Freddy looking for different birds. *"There's a barn owl,"* Freddy said, pointing overhead. *"Linnet, what's the species?"*

"Tyto Alba," I replied, while I was studying the wooden ceiling.

"Good girl," he said, *"That's my encyclopedic genius. I'm so proud of you."*

Thea had come along on the walk as well. She was holding my hand. *"We're both proud of you,"* she echoed Freddy, *"and before you know it, we'll be together again."*

I took their photograph down from the dresser. I wished that I were on the picture too. How happy and full of cheer they both looked. There was a great desire in me to speak with them, to ask them things, to tell them things; but my greatest desire of all was just to sit between them and lean my head into their sides like I used to do.

A little rustling at my feet lifted me away from the empty feeling threatening to overwhelm me. Glancing down I saw the tiny, grey mouse disappear under my cot. It had lived there since I'd moved in, now scurrying here, now running there, but always in the last instance returning to take refuge under my cot. Dropping the photograph on the coverlet, I pulled up my feet, lay on my stomach and hung my head over the edge of the bed. Sure enough, it was there, sitting on its hind feet, its little forepaws folded on its chest.

"Hi," I whispered ever so soft, "Hi, little mouse." He sat quietly, gazing fixedly at me with his beady eyes. He was not as talkative as the parakeet.

"I think I'll call you Freda," I murmured, "That's for Freddy and Thea. Do you like that?"

The little creature did not stir but his ears did perk up a bit.

"I think that I will sneak downstairs," I kept talking, "and see if I can take some raisins from the container in the bakery. Do you like raisins, Freda?"

Very carefully I lifted my head, quietly sat up, put my feet down on the floor and then inched my way over to the stairwell. Would I be able to get downstairs without *Pake* and *Tante* Adri hearing me? Considering that my socks made less noise than my shoes, halfway down the first stairs I took them off and placed them neatly, side by side, on one of the steps. Reaching the first hallway, the snorting sounds of both *Pake* and *Tante* Adri helped me relax. They were not likely to come out any time soon to ask me what I was doing. Reaching the front store bakery room, I tried very hard to remember where it was that I had seen *Pake* take out raisins when he was making raisin bread. Pulling open several drawers behind the counter, I was pleased to find a large plastic bag full of the little fruits. A few would surely be enough. But I had no pocket. If only I were a German soldier wearing a grey-green uniform! Well, my hand would have to be my pocket. Carefully I reached for the bag. It was unopened. I pulled and tugged and suddenly there was a hole, a rip, a most fearful tear. Perhaps *Pake* wouldn't notice. *And do ducks know how to fly*, I heard Karel say. Well, since the bag was ripped open now anyway, I was determined to carry some raisins up to Freda.

Shaking out a few, I meticulously folded over the gaping rip, laying the bag back into the drawer so that the tear didn't show. A speedy retreat from the kitchen followed. The eighth stair creaked ominously as I hurried up. In my hurry I had forgotten to step over it. I froze for a moment. But the snoring continued in full process. My shoes smiled at me on the second set of stairs and I smiled back, depositing my handful of raisins into the right shoe.

"Now then, Freda," I began, as soon as I emerged from the stairwell, "just see what Linnet has brought you."

But when I looked under the bed, Freda had gone. I hid the raisins in the first drawer of the dresser, right between my stack of undies and next to the roll of licorice. But one of the raisins I placed under the bed, hoping that the little, grey-haired mouse would come back.

****

I had asked *Tante* Adri if I might feed Ko every day after I had completed my sweeping, dusting, mopping, and Bible copying. She was agreeable to the idea, but emphasized heavily that I should be careful not to spill any birdseed on the floor or on the bed. Ko was the name of the little green parakeet. It soon became my absolute favorite job to make sure that his small feeder was full and every now and then *Tante* Adri let me put some fruit into his cage as well. Ko was fond of me. I knew this was so because he chirped when I was there. Often when he observed me, he lowered his head with its little tuft on top onto his green shoulder. One of my books had a small section on parakeets and I carefully examined the pages which dealt with taming them. People should not be too quick about taming them, the book cautioned, because gentling parakeets is time–consuming. A person's hands are almost as big as a parakeet's tiny body so you should begin befriending a parakeet by showing it your hand every day. I found this good and sensible advice. Every day after I poured a little seed into Ko's small dish, I held up my hand and stood like a sentinel until my hand got tired. I talked to him too and gave him information, information and knowledge that I had recently acquired. After all, he never left the bedroom and very likely never heard much about what was going on in the world.

"Hello, Ko. How are you today?"

He chirped back, *Fine, Linnet.*

"That good, Ko. Did you know, by the way, that you were made on the fifth day by God?"

Ko's cheeping told me that he had rarely thought about when he had been made, and that he had no idea that he had been made on the fifth day. I told him I had never thought about it either.

"You were made on the same day as the fish, Ko. Did you know that and did you look at the fish as you flew over the water?"

Ko tweeted thoughtfully. And I could understand that. I was thoughtful too. I wondered if all the birds had gotten along on that day. The eagle and the finch, the wren and the falcon – had they all been thrown into the sky at the same time by God? Or one by one?

"Well, never mind, Ko. We can talk about it the next time I visit. I'm feeling fine today, although I really miss Freddy and Thea. But I'm so happy to see you and they would love you. Do you think you would like them too?"

Ko put his little beak on his shoulder and preened, chirruping softly.

"That's wonderful Ko. How does the seed taste today?"

He replied with a loud chirp.

Fine. It tastes fine. But the best thing I'm tasting is that you're here with me, Linnet.

"Shall I dance for you, Ko?"

Yes, please Linnet. That would be wonderful. You know what I would really like though, Linnet?

"What, Ko?"

Well, I would really like to see you jump on the bed. I've never seen a person jump on a bed.

I put my right hand, the hand I had been holding up in front of the cage, down. The truth was that Thea and Freddy never let me jump on their bed and my attic cot was much too small for jumping up and down. *Pake* and Tante Adri's bed was an open invitation. Great and downy–like, it seemed to beg me to test its buoyancy and within me there was an enormous hankering for a jolly good jump.

"Well, if you really want me to, Ko, I could bounce just once or twice."

Ko chirped agreeably and I meandered around the bed, feeling the white bedspread with my fingers. They sank into the fleecy material and almost disappeared into the coverlet.

"It's very soft, Ko."

"All the better to jump on," he chirped back supportively.

So I took off my shoes and climbed onto the bed. It felt like sitting on the crest of a wave coming down. It felt wonderful. I bounced an itsy-bit at first and then, turning on my hands and knees, carefully stood up. Swaying like the bushes by the Wadden Sea, I began to rebound in earnest. Up I went and down I came – up I went and down I came – again and again. I spread my arms out like the wings of an eagle and soared.

"You are amazing," chirped Ko and I agreed.

Leaping with greater and greater abandon, I did not hear the door open but the horrified shriek of *Tante* Adri did reach my ears and did stop me short just as I was reaching for the clouds on the ceiling.

"What in tarnation is going on here?"

"Uh," were all the words I could manage, and I came down flat in the four-poster bed with a depressing flump.

"Get off!!"

Tante Adri's voice was not getting any less shrill. I sat up, stretched my stocking feet over the edge of the bed and slid down onto the floor. Ko was remarkably quiet, not chirping at all any longer. *Tante* Adri plodded over to the bed and began smoothing out the coverlet with her hands, all the while breathing heavily.

"I'm sorry," I managed weakly, and to be sure I was.

"You will go to your room. You will not have lunch. And to think that this very afternoon I arranged for you to begin sewing lessons at Sanne's house."

"I'm really sorry, *Tante* Adri."

"Go."

I went, but first I picked up my shoes. They were under Ko's cage. He chirped at this point and said, *"I'm sorry, Linnet. We were just beginning to have such a good time."*

Then I was out the door, in the hall, and up the stairs. I cried for a bit on my cot, and then took out my bird books. I turned to the pages on parakeets and reread the part about how to tame them to sit on your finger. Maybe I could coach Ko to sit on mine as he was probably used to the size of my hand by now.

Extend your index finger and place it in front of the bird's breast. Slowly and gently press your finger against the breast sideways, and say 'Up'. His instinct will be to step onto your finger and use it as a perch. When he does this give him a treat.

Surely I would be able to teach Ko to sit on my finger. But maybe Tante Adri would never let me into her bedroom after this disaster. I sniffled afresh and then fell asleep. I woke up to footsteps coming up the stairs. Immediately sitting up, I anxiously studied the stairwell. But it was not *Tante* Adri's head which appeared, but *Pake's*.

"Hello, Linnet."

He did not seem angry. Maybe he hadn't spoken to *Tante* Adri yet. Cautiously I smiled at him.

"Hello, *Pake*."

"I understand you did a little jumping?"

Ashamed, I hung my head. *Pake* began to speak. He was a bit disjointed but the general message was clear.

"Linnet, maybe you can make up for your . . . for your misbehavior by going next door right now for a sewing lesson and by trying very hard to learn how to sew. Sanne, our neighbor, called on *Tante* Adri this morning to say that she would like to meet you. *Tante* Adri is . . . she is a little out of sorts right now. That is why I came up to get you."

He stopped, clearly at a loss as to what else to say, and I understood that *Tante* Adri was, at this point, unwilling to speak to me herself.

"Yes, *Pake*."

He disappeared down the stairs and I put the books back in their drawer, slipped into my shoes, did up the laces, and slowly made my way down to the shop. *Tante* Adri was standing behind the counter as I came in. Serving a customer, she pointedly turned her back to me not saying one word. *Pake*, who was mixing flour at the sideboard, called out.

"Sanne lives in the house next door to us. She lives to the left, Linnet. You should be able to find it."

I nodded and exited the bakery. The copper bell rang out as I left, but it sounded rather somber.

It was a late October afternoon. I had been here some three months plus, now. That was a very long time! A grade school, a few streets over, spilled voices into our lane from its schoolyard. I had no desire to attend a school. Freddy and Thea had talked about sending me to the island school next year, but who knew if that would happen? Without thinking about where I was going, I walked right by the house left of the bakery, but a sharp tapping on the window stopped me short. A lady, an old, gray-haired lady, stood behind the window, gesturing and pointing me over to her front door. I smiled, bobbing my head up and down to show her I understood, and marched over. The door opened almost immediately.

"Hello, you must be Linnet." A wrinkled, cheerful face regarded me.

"Yes, I am."

"Well, you must come in, Linnet." She stood aside and waved me in. "I'm Sanne, and you may call me Oma Sanne, if you like."

I did like that. Oma Sanne sounded friendly and it made me feel good to meet someone whom Freddy had liked and of whom he had spoken the last day I saw him. Suddenly, I felt genuinely sad. Just to think about Freddy and about not having seen either him or Thea for weeks and weeks put a lump in my throat.

"Well, you have no coat to hang up, so you might as well step straight into my living room." I followed her, swallowing the lump away as I walked. "You can sit over there, Linnet, on the couch and I'll sit right next to you."

Oma Sanne was short, about the same size as Thea. Her hair was silvery-gray and softly wreathed a wrinkled face. Her eyes were red-rimmed and a bit watery, as if she read too much in the dark. That's what Thea had always said would happen to my eyes if I read without a light in bed after she had gone downstairs.

"Are you comfortable, Child? Your feet don't quite reach the floor, do they? You can curl them up on the couch if you like."

I tucked my feet under me and leaned back into the soft sofa. It was almost as soft as *Pake* and *Tante* Adri's bed. What would Oma Sanne say if I stood up and jumped on her couch?

"That's right, Linnet. Get comfortable and then tell me all about yourself. What have you been doing next door?" Oma Sanne's voice was very kind. No wonder Freddy had liked coming here.

"Did you know Freddy?" I blurted out.

"Freddy?" Oma Sanne responded, and then went on. "Oh, Freddy. Why yes, I knew him very well. I think that boy was born tall, and he could certainly reach the floor when he sat on this couch. As a matter of fact, he always stretched his feet out under that table almost tipping it over."

There was a small coffee table in front of the chesterfield, and I could easily imagine that Freddy had extended his long legs under it. I smiled at Oma Sanne.

"Well, if that isn't the most beautiful smile," she said, "and I wager that the mouth holding that smile would like a cup of tea."

I nodded, and tears filled my eyes at the same time. No one had said such kind and personal words to me since I had arrived. *Pake* smiled at me and *Tante* Adri fed me, but no one had spoken to me or asked me questions. Karel had not been back. Perhaps he was just too busy. But the truth of it was that I was terribly lonely.

"Now then," Oma Sanne chided mildly, "tears on my couch and on your very first visit? I hope that you don't dislike me already."

I shook my head and sniffed as my nose was beginning to run. Oma tucked an embroidered hanky into my hand.

"Here, child," Oma went on, "don't mind my silly words. Have a good cry, and afterwards we'll have a little chin-wag. Now I'll just go and make us a nice cup of tea."

She got up and bustled through the room, disappearing around a corner behind which I presumed there was a kitchen. I heard water run and the clatter of cups being set down, the way I used to hear Freddy messing about in the kitchen when Thea was putting me to bed. Blowing my nose, I began to relax. It was a nice room. There were some geraniums on the window sill and a bookcase with lots of books lined almost an entire wall.

"Do you like *koek*, Linnet?"

I managed to call out "Yes, please," even as I blew my nose again. No wonder that Freddy had liked Sanne. She was nice and I was so hungry. Leaning my head against the back of the couch, I closed my eyes. It was almost, almost like being back home in the cottage. I wondered if Thea had ever been here. I knew that she had not been to the bakery, but maybe Freddy had taken her to visit Oma Sanne.

Surely Oma would have taken to Thea. And Thea would have liked Oma too. Maybe Freddy and Thea would come to get me soon. Maybe today, or maybe tomorrow. I had promised to help *Pake* tomorrow, though—had promised to help him put some tape on the bakery window and on the window in the dining room.

"Planes flying around," *Pake* had informed me, "shaking the ground. Other stores, and houses as well, are taping up whole sections of their windows. That way, if there's an explosion from something or other, the glass won't shatter."

"Sure, *Pake*."

So perhaps they would come after I helped *Pake*, and they would be so surprised that I had helped with such an important chore as taping up windows.

"Well, Linnet," Oma Sanne's voice shook me out of my daydreaming, "here's a nice cup of hot tea and some *koek* to go with it."

It was *koek* just like the kind I used to buy for Thea on the island. *Pake*'s bakery didn't have it, so he probably didn't make it. I don't know why, because I was convinced that everyone in the whole world liked *koek*.

"Thank you, Oma Sanne," I said politely.

"Well, there's a good girl," she beamed, "so well-mannered. Now Freddy, he wasn't always polite."

"No?"

"And that boy could eat. Why, he'd eat three pieces of *koek* in one visit."

I was flabbergasted. Not so much that Freddy could eat that much, but that Oma Sanne had obviously let him eat that much. Oma put the tray she was carrying on the coffee table and sat down next to me.

"Now we'll have a grand tea-time," she mapped out, "and then we'll talk about your troubles."

Not waiting for a response, she asked if I liked dogs. "Well," I answered, my mouth full of *koek* by this time, "I actually really like cats and birds."

"That could be a problem," she wryly grinned, "because those two don't get on together."

"Well, we had a cat," I told her, "and her name was Belle. She wore a bell, you see, because that would warn the birds that she was coming."

Oma laughed and remarked, "Now that was a good idea. Was it yours?"

"No, actually it was Thea's," I said, and was suddenly thrown back into the time when Thea had carefully fitted a collar with the small bell around Belle's neck.

"I see," Oma replied, noting the cloud that was settling over my face again. "Thea sounds like a very smart person."

"Oh, yes," I eagerly responded, "she is. And do you know her, Oma?"

"I do in a way," Oma replied softly. "You see, I was only told about her by Freddy and . . . ."

"And who else?" I questioned.

"Well, that doesn't really matter," Oma said. "I just know that Freddy really loves her, and because of that I love her too."

I sighed a big sigh of relief and felt a warm, a very warm feeling in my heart. All this time living here and not being able to speak about my Thea, my very own Thea, was so very difficult.

"Freddy told me," and I studied Oma Sanne's face very carefully as I spoke, "that *Pake* and *Tante* Adri don't like Thea and . . . ."

I stopped. I'd said it. I'd repeated that awful sentence that had been hounding me ever since I came here. *Pake and Tante Adri don't like Thea.* There was quiet in Oma Sanne's room except for the clock that hung behind the couch. It ticked and ticked. *"Thea. Freddy. Thea. Freddy."*

Oma's eyes did not shy away from meeting my gaze. "Linnet," she said, her eyes full of compassion, "there are some things that are very difficult to explain."

"Freddy told me," I persisted, "that if I should ever be lonely or wanted to talk to someone, that I should go to you."

She smiled, picked up her teacup and slowly sipped the hot liquid. I took another bite of my *koek*.

"He was right," she answered me a moment later as she put down her cup repeating, "Of course, he was right. You may always come here, Linnet. I'm just sorry that I didn't know you were here until *Tante* Adri stopped by yesterday to ask about sewing. I immediately went back this morning and told her that today was a good day."

"But I've been here a long, long time."

"You know," she rejoined, looking at me keenly, "if Freddy told you about me, you might have come earlier as well. You might have asked *Pake* and *Tante* Adri where I lived and if you could visit me."

I blushed. She was right. Perhaps now she would not like me any more because I had not looked her up sooner, because I had blamed Freddy's father and stepmother. Maybe she missed Freddy too.

"I'm sorry," I mumbled.

Oma Sanne moved closer to me and put her arm around my shoulder. "You know," she said, "it's a good thing to reserve judgment until you know all the details about something; until you know exactly what happened in a certain situation."

"What happened then," I responded weakly, "what happened so that Freddy and Thea never came here?"

"Yes," she said, "now that is the question. I can tell you some of the answer, but not all of it."

I sat up straight and regarded her, even as I felt her rub the tension out of my neck with her hand.

"It was a long time ago, Linnet," she went on, "and sometimes people dig themselves into a hole by hanging on to something that they are sorry for later. But because they have taken a position, they refuse to go back and say that they were wrong, that they didn't mean what they said."

"What," I asked, "was said? Did Freddy say something bad?"

"Well," Oma smiled, "I suppose the only thing he said was that he was going to marry Thea."

"What was the matter with that?" I demanded.

"Nothing," Oma answered sadly, "except that she was Jewish."

"Jewish? What is Jewish, Oma?"

Oma took her hand away and shrugged. She seemed unhappy. "I suppose being Jewish in the strictest sense of the word is simply being a human being – a human being like you and like me. But if you define being Jewish by race, well then it would be someone who belonged to the race of Abraham, Isaac, and Jacob."

"I have copied chapters that talked about Abraham."

"Copied chapters?"

"Yes, every day after I sweep the kitchen and the shop, I have to write down a chapter in the Bible."

"I see," Oma commented, "but I don't really see. Why is it that you have to write down a chapter of the Bible every day? And can you do that? How old are you, Linnet?"

"I'm five, but I'll be six in January," I replied rather proudly, "and Thea and Freddy taught me how to read and write. But I can't print very quickly yet. *Pake* and *Tante* Adri know that we didn't read the Bible on the island, so they want me to learn what is in it."

Actually, what I told Oma wasn't quite true. *Pake* and Tante Adri had never asked me again if we read the Bible after that first meal. But Tante Adri had quizzed me with questions like, "Who was the first man?" and "Where did he live?" and "What is sin?" I had failed the answers miserably, judging from the way she clucked her tongue.

"Are you learning anything, Linnet?"

"Well," I replied, "the birds were made on the fifth day. You see I really like birds and ..."

Had I learned anything else?

"Does *Tante* Adri read the chapter with you later and explain what you are reading?" Oma Sanne's voice had increased in volume. "Well, she corrects me when I pronounce a word wrong, and there are a lot of words I don't know. But I do think it is all very interesting."

"Linnet, when you come here the next time for sewing, and we will be doing some, well, then I will read you some Bible stories and we'll see if we can't talk about some of these interesting things."

"So what is Jewish?"

I did want to get back to the problem of Freddy and Thea not coming here.

"It is difficult for me to explain that to you, Linnet, without telling you about what is written in the Bible. I would very much like to do that though."

I turned my body towards her. "Is it a bad thing to be Jewish, Oma. Is it wrong?"

"No, Linnet. It is not a bad thing to be Jewish and it is certainly not wrong. But there are some people who think that it is wrong. Those people are wicked."

"Are *Pake* and *Tante* Adri wicked then?"

"I think that *Pake* and *Tante* Adri, especially Tante Adri, have a wrong understanding of what it is to be . . . ."

She stopped.

"Are they taking you to church, Linnet?"

"Yes, they do."

"And how do you like that?"

"Well, I have to sit very quietly. There are a lot of people there and a man goes to the front and climbs a stairs and stands on a high platform and talks."

"Do you understand what he says?"

"Well, I can hear him fine. But I don't always understand what he is talking about, Oma."

Oma sighed.

"Oma Sanne," I asked, changing the subject drastically. "Do you think that Freddy and Thea will come here soon to take me home again?"

She picked up her teacup again and offered me another piece of *koek*. "I'm afraid it might be a little while yet, Linnet. But I will tell you that I am very happy that they have not come yet, because now I've had a chance to meet you. You'll have to be very brave. We are entering, I believe, a very dark part of history."

"And darkness was upon the face of the deep," I quipped, recalling verbatim my writing out that part of the first chapter of the Bible."

"Yes," Oma smiled now, "but it's very important to remember what comes after that, Linnet. *"And the Spirit of God moved upon the face of the waters."*

10

My time of learning with Oma Sanne began in earnest. The consent of *Pake* and *Tante* Adri had not been easily obtained. After a long consultation (a consultation from which I was excluded), permission was given to Oma, who used to be a teacher, to coach me in both printing and cursive writing, as well as sewing, Bible, and arithmetic. Although initially, *Tante* Adri was quite exasperated about the fact that it might seem to neighbors that she was falling short with regard to my education, in the end she capitulated. The truth was that spending time with me was not her favorite activity.

My periods of schooling with Oma Sanne were to be every day – every day from ten in the morning until three in the afternoon. I was to eat lunch with Oma and I was also to help her with cleaning, gardening, and any other tasks she might need done. *Pake* informed me of this a few days after my initial visit with Oma. He called me over after I had swept and sopped the bakery floor. It happened to be during a time when *Tante* Adri had gone out to run a few errands. Inspecting my work, *Pake* concluded that I had done a fine job. Then he went on to tell me that, from now on, I would regularly be going next door for lessons with Oma Sanne. But, he expanded, there were conditions.

"Before you leave for *Mevrouw* every morning," *Pake* emphasized in his dry voice, "you are first to complete your chores here as you have done every morning."

I nodded vigorously, trying very hard not to show him how very excited I was, simultaneously endeavoring to show him goodwill.

"All right, Child," he went on, "you can stop bobbing your head up and down. That's settled then. I trust you will do your very best. As well, if I need help delivering bread in town, I might call on you to come with me during the day without any protest on your part."

My nodding at this was a little more subdued. The truth was that in the course of the last few weeks, I had thoroughly enjoyed the extra chore of going with *Pake* to supply regular customers with bakery products. I was getting to know some of the people in the town. Riding on the back of *Pake*'s delivery bicycle was fun. He handed me packages when he stopped and I'd have to run up to doors to hand them over to customers, collect the money they owed and take it back to him.

At the completion of *Pake's* admonition to do my very best in all the work assigned to me, however, he gently appended the fact that he was missing some raisins. At this point, he studied my face very carefully. Miserably aware that my cheeks were turning enormously red, I examined my shoes. Surely now he would cancel his permission for me to go to Oma Sanne's. Still, I felt compelled to admit guilt. Freddy and Thea had ingrained truthfulness in me, and woe if I was caught by them in an untruth.

Consequently, with my eyes glued to the bakery floor, I confessed that there was a mouse who lived under my cot and that I was attempting to train the little grey animal by feeding it raisins. *Pake* made no comment during this revelation, and when I felt courageous enough to lift my eyes up to his face, I was amazed to see the faintest glimmer of a smile in his green eyes.

"The next time, Linnet," he said, "the next time just ask me for some raisins."

"Yes, *Pake*," I promised, breathing in deeply.

"Go on, then," he finished, "you are done here for today. Go on to *Mevrouw,* Mrs. Smit, only be sure to put the broom away first and to wash your hands after that."

"Yes, *Pake*," I breathed out again, and without heeding what he had just said, immediately ran out the bakery door with the broom in my hand and without my coat. Shamefacedly, I came back in a moment later and leaned the broom in its corner.

"Now wash your hands, Linnet," *Pake* called out from the other room, where he was taking bread out of the oven.

"Yes, *Pake*."

Helter skelter, I dashed up the stairs to the small W.C., vigorously scrubbing my hands over the sink, spattering soap suds all over the edge, unable to contain my excitement. But afterwards, as I was about to race down the stairs again, I heard Ko chirp. Swiveling about on my heels, I stole over to say hello to him. I'd been banned from *Tante* Adri's room, but she had gone out and the parakeet probably missed me awfully. On guard, I opened the door a hairline crack.

"Hello, Ko," I whispered.

"Hello, Linnet," he chirped. *"Where have you been?"*

"Well, remember that I jumped on the bed the last time I was here?"

"I do."

"Well, *Tante* Adri didn't like that, and she doesn't want me in her bedroom anymore. So right now, I can't visit you. But maybe," I added quickly, not wanting to depress him, "maybe she will change her mind about it."

"I hope so," Ko cheeped, and preened his left wing.

"Yes," I agreed, "and now, Ko, I'm going to our neighbor, to Oma Sanne, and she's going to teach me lots of things. But most of all, Ko, you'll never guess what she told me about Thea."

"What?" Ko chirruped, lifting his head and peering at me with his beady eyes.

"Well, she told me that Thea was Jewish. And I don't know what that is yet, but when I find out, maybe it will help bring her here. Wouldn't that be wonderful!!"

Ko had no words for that bit of information and just grinned, his little beak chuckling with chirrups.

"Well, goodbye, Ko. I'll be back as soon as the coast is clear again."

"Goodbye, Linnet."

I hop-skipped down the stairs and laughed when the eighth step creaked. I took my coat off the coat rack and put it on.

"Goodbye, *Pake*."

"Goodbye, Linnet."

Oma Sanne greeted me with a big smile. "Well, and here's my favorite pupil and my only pupil, Linnet Veerman, reporting for her first day of class. And how are you this morning, Linnet?"

"Fine, Oma."

I was shy all of a sudden. After my tremendous burst of eager energy, apprehension gripped my heart. What if Oma found out that she didn't like me? What if I wasn't able to live up to her expectations of learning? What if . . . ? And then Thea's voice rang through my mind. *"You are asking too many questions, Little Thing. Slow down."*

"All right, Thea," I whispered to myself. "All right."

"Well, are you going to stand outside all day? Then we won't get a lick done. So please come in. I'm so glad you're here because I was just a bit lonely."

Oma's voice was lighthearted, and I could tell she was trying to put me at ease. I smiled, wiped my feet on the doormat, walked in, took off my coat and hung it on the clothes tree standing in her foyer.

"Did you have a good sleep last night, Linnet?"

Actually, I hadn't slept that well. I had attempted to get Freda to eat out of my hand without any success. Keeping some crumbs from the bread at lunch time in my pocket, I had been unable to cajole the little creature to venture close to my hands, even though I had sat ever so quiet. Then I had tried to pretend that I was back home on the island, that Thea had snugly tucked me into my cot – but that hadn't worked very well either. The wooden timber beams over my head had seemed oppressive and grim. It was as if the ceiling was closing in on me. Eventually I'd gotten up and walked over to the round window. It was cleaner now, scrubbed with some soapy water and dried with one of the rags I used on the bakery floor. But nonetheless the pane was hazy and difficult to see through especially in the twilight.

I longed to hear Freddy make tea – to hear the tinkle of cups as he and Thea sat on the couch, talking in low tones. But there was only stillness. I knew that *Pake* and Tante Adri were in the kitchen, but the kitchen was two floors below and I could not discern even a murmur of their voices.

Wandering over to the small closet across from the window at the other end of the room, I contemplated shadows. It wasn't a closet really, only a closed off area which for some reason had been separated from the rest of the attic. Containing a chest, a metal bar with some hangers dangling from it, a skylight in the slanted roof above let in the night. Stars twinkled through the skylight, and the stars did comfort me some. I had sat on the chest and had regarded the vastness of the heavens. And the stars had blinked on my thoughts, thoughts of Freddy and Thea, thoughts about what they were doing and if they missed me. It was on the fourth day that God had made the stars. So the stars were older than birds – older by a whole day. Did Freddy know that?

"So, did you have a good sleep, little day-dreamer?"

Oma's voice brought me back to the present, to her foyer where I was standing.

"Sure."

"Well, it sounds and looks as if you could use a nap later, perhaps at the same time when I nap. Oh well, we'll figure it out, you and I, Linnet."

Oma had a way with her that made you comfortable. Being in her company was a bit like wearing a comfortable sweater. I was wearing a sweater that Thea had knit and that embraced me too. Walking ahead of me into the dining room, not even bothering to see if I would follow, Oma Sanne intimated that I belonged in her home. The couch already looked familiar and hailed me. But it was not the couch to which we walked but the table – a table which had several books lying on it.

"Now then, Linnet, what is it to be? Shall we have a Bible story first, or shall we do some schoolwork – some adding and subtracting? Keep in mind that we have lots and lots of time and that it's our first day. We'll establish a routine as we go, so it doesn't matter what you choose right now."

Oma sat down on one of the chairs by the table and patted the one on her left for me to sit on. A Bible story sounded inviting and I told her so.

"This," Oma went on, pulling a black covered book towards her, "is a Bible. I don't suppose that you have a Bible, Linnet?"

"No," I answered as I sat down. "I don't."

"Well, no matter," she said. "I will give you one, and it will be your very own. That way you can read a bit before you go to sleep every night. *Pake* and Tante Adri say you can read very well."

I did not know what to say to that.

"But before we begin each day together," Oma went on, "I do want to say that there will be one thing which will be the same each day. And that is that we will begin with prayer."

I thought of *Pake* and *Tante* Adri. *"Fold your hands and close your eyes."* I did it in church too, and found prayer, especially the long prayer, a time during which I could relax and dream about the island. The only tricky part was keeping a sharp ear out for the word "Amen."

"Do you know what prayer is, Linnet?"

"A time when you fold your hands and close your eyes."

"Yes, you usually do that," she answered, "but to whom are you speaking when you do that?"

I hunted for an answer, but the truth was that I didn't really know. I shook my head and looked at Oma rather helplessly. She smiled.

"Well, then, that's where we'll start. We'll start by talking about prayer and what that means. But before we do that, I'd like to ask God to help me explain it to you. I'd like to ask Him to open your eyes, so that you will see Him."

Oma folded her hands, bowed her head, and she closed her eyes. My eyes were wide open. Didn't Oma mean that she hoped mine would be closed just as hers were closed? I sat quietly and listened to the clock on Oma's mantel ticking away. Her prayer flowed through the minutes and then she opened her eyes and began to talk.

"It is true that people fold their hands and close their eyes when they pray. But, Linnet, the talking people do while they sit with folded hands and closed eyes is to someone. They are speaking to God."

It was quiet for a moment and I remembered Jürgen sitting in the dunes. I remembered that he had told me that God had given him a family. Had he talked to God and asked Him for a family? Willem's words came back to me. When I had asked him if God was in the boat, he had said: *"I should say so, child, for God is everywhere."* I repeated Willem's words.

"God is everywhere, isn't He?"

Oma smiled. "Yes, Linnet, that is a great truth. And how do you know that?"

"Well, someone told me."

"Who?"

I supposed that it would be all right to tell Oma about Jürgen and also about Willem. After all, Jürgen was on the island and he didn't know Oma or where she lived. So I began by telling her about my walk in the dunes that last day, and how I had tripped over a leg, and how that leg had turned out to be a German soldier, and that his name was Jůrgen.

"He was very nice, Oma. He showed me a picture of his family, of his little girl, and her name was Emma, just like me."

"Just like you?" Oma interrupted, "But your name is not Emma, but Linnet."

So I explained how I had worried about telling the soldier my real name and that I had used the name Emma because Freddy had just told me a story about a dog called Emma. And that the name Emma had pleased Jůrgen very much, because his daughter had been called Emma as well.

"Providence," Oma said as she leaned back in her chair, "that was providence, Child."

"Providence," I repeated, "is that another name for God?"

Oma sighed. "Linnet you have many good questions. Why don't you tell me first what else happened with Jůrgen."

"Well, Jůrgen told me that God had given him his family. So I asked him who God was."

I went on to tell her what Jůrgen had answered and that this was the first time I had ever heard of God. Oma sighed many times during the course of my story, which grew longer because I went on to narrate what happened when I got back and how I had to wear the black cloak that Thea had made for me. At intervals in my narration, Oma exclaimed, "Linnet! Linnet!" or "Child! Child!" And when I got to the part where Thea and I had thrown ourselves face down in the sand hardly daring to breathe for fear of being discovered, while Freddy had greeted a German soldier on the path, she hugged me. At the end of my story, and I stopped at the part where Karel had left me at the bakery, she gave me another hug.

"And now you are here," she murmured, "and I am so thankful that you arrived safely in Steendorp."

"Did you know that I lived on the island with Freddy and Thea?"

"Well, not really. Freddy hasn't come to visit me anymore, you see. When your *Pake* and *Tante* Adri said he could not come home with Thea, he stayed away from our town. I missed him, but I understood that he could not leave his wife, your Thea."

I was glad that Oma said that about Thea.

"So, Linnet, back to the question of who God is. Remember the first chapter of the Bible? The chapter you had to copy for *Pake* and *Tante* Adri?"

"Yes, I do."

"You were very good in remembering that the birds were made on the fifth day. But I'd like to go back to before what was made on all the days. I'd like to go back to the very first words of the Bible. Do you by any chance remember what those words were?"

I thought very hard and then shook my head.

"No, I can't remember, Oma."

She opened the Bible and made me review those first four words.

"In the beginning God," I read.

"Yes," Oma said, "and those words tell us a lot about who God is."

I suppose I appeared a little muddled, because she smiled at me reassuringly.

"Linnet, I'm so glad I am your neighbor and that I'm getting to know you. You've had quite a journey getting here, but you are here safely. God has taken such care of you and I think that God has chosen you to be one of His lambs."

Her words only mystified me even more. I had seen lambs on the island. Freddy and I had tramped many lanes together looking for birds, and we'd passed farmers' fields and had seen lambs in the springtime. They were so fun to watch. Little stick–like legs, jumping and bouncing with abandon, with even more abandon than I had shown when I had jumped on *Tante* Adri's bed and had leaped all over the place. But puzzlement as to myself being a lamb made me repeat the word.

"Lambs?"

"Yes, but we'll talk about that some other time," Oma continued. "First, back to the first four words of the Bible. *"In the beginning God."* These are very important words, Linnet. I think you've probably heard or read fairy tales and you might remember that they often start with *'Once upon a time.'"*

I nodded. What Oma said was true. Most fairy tales did start that way, and often Freddy and Thea started stories that way as well.

"Well, notice that the Bible starts not with *"Once upon a time"* but with *"In the beginning God."* You see, Linnet, in the beginning there was no time. There were no hours, no minutes, and no seconds. But God was. The words *"In the beginning God"* are very important and very awesome. They introduce us to the idea of no time. And," Oma added, "it is very difficult for us to imagine no time."

The clock on the mantel was ticking through Oma's words. She was right. It was very hard for me to imagine no time. There was a time to get up in the morning and a time to go to sleep at night. There was a time to eat lunch and a time to sweep the floor. There had been the time when I left the island and the time that I came here.

"So God is 'no time'?" I asked.

"A better way to put it is that He is outside of time."

I thought about that and the ideas and sentences that jumped around in my mind from that sentence all got entangled in each other. I shook my head.

"I can't understand it, Oma."

"I think no one can, Child. It's just something you have to believe. Now I want you to read the next word, the fifth word in the Bible."

So I read, *"created."*

"Do you know what it means to create, Linnet?"

"Well, yes, I do," I answered, and happy I was that I did know the answer to this question. "You see Thea draws pictures and she paints and often before she does that she often says 'I am feeling creative today' or 'I think I'll create something now'. And then she'll go and pick up her easel and set up it in the yard, or she'll set it up in the kitchen if it's too cold outside. Then she'll draw a beautiful picture, Oma."

"Does she use paint and brushes?"

"Oh, yes," I went on eagerly, glad to speak of my Thea, "she has lots of paints and brushes. And she has a wooden easel that Freddy made for her."

"Well," Oma went on, "God created beauty, but He did not need either paint or brushes. Neither did He use wood such as Freddy might have used to make Thea her easel."

"What did He use, Oma?" I was curious.

"He used Himself. He used His voice. That is to say, He spoke."

"He spoke?"

"Let's read the whole first chapter, Linnet, and whenever we hear God speaking, we'll stop and together we'll think about what He is saying or what He is making."

So we did. We read the whole first chapter of the Bible together and we stopped at different places to talk about what was happening, about what was being created. The truth was that whereas before when I had copied out the chapter for *Pake* and Tante Adri, there had only been words, difficult words. Now these words were deciphered into understanding. With Oma, I was beginning to see, to comprehend to some degree, what I was reciting. I could see the island, the sand, the sky, and the birds; I could feel the wind and the leaves on the bushes; and I began to grasp in some small measure that the Bible was telling me that God had made all these things.

"Will God ever say anything else, Oma? Does He ever make new things?"

"Yes, I think He does, Linnet. But first we're going to read the second chapter together."

And that is what we did.

"Now, Linnet," Oma said, even as she got up from her chair, "I'm going to the kitchen to fix our lunch, but I want you to read the chapter again by yourself, and I want you to write down in this notebook that I'm giving you, any questions you might think of or any thoughts that you might have as you read."

"But Oma," I said, "now that I know who God is, and now that I know that He made everything, can't I pray to Him like you said at the beginning?"

Oma sat down again. "Yes, of course you can, Linnet," she answered. "Is there something special you want to say?"

"Well, I would like to ask God to make the war stop," I said, "because to make something stop is making something too, isn't it? And I would like to ask him to make Freddy and Thea come here. And I would like to ask Him to make *Pake* and Tante Adri like Thea. Can He do all those things if I ask Him nicely, Oma?"

"Sometimes," Oma said, "sometimes when someone makes us a present of something new, we want to use it right away without reading the instructions."

She stopped and I remembered that a long time ago, Thea had told me that she would teach me how to swim. I had been so excited, that the moment we reached the seashore, I had not waited for her instructions but had run into the water all by myself. Tripping over my legs in my excitement to swim, I had fallen facedown and had swallowed a good deal of the Wadden Sea before Thea had picked me up and carried me back to the shore.

"Foolish little girl," she had chided, "for not waiting for me to teach you."

I remembered the incident very clearly. Later, I had learned to swim, but that was after quite a few instructive sessions with Thea and Freddy.

"Yes, Oma," I said, "I know. But can we have a first prayer now? And can you show me how to begin?"

"Of course, we can, Linnet," she answered, folding my hands into hers, "and perhaps I can start and you can finish."

So Oma began.

"Dear Father," she began, and that was something I didn't know, that you could call God "Father."

"We would like to come to You to praise You for making the whole world around us. For making the flowers, the trees, the sun, moon and stars, the birds, the fish, and all the animals. We know You made them, because You told us this in the Bible. We thank you also, dear Father, for making people. We thank you for making us."

I understood all the things for which she thanked God. I loved all those things very much. I surely would be able to pray like that.

"Thank you for Linnet, Father," she went on. "Thank you for bringing her into my life. Please Father, open the eyes of her heart so that she may believe everything she reads about You in the Bible. Please take care of Freddy and Thea wherever they are, and also watch out for *Pake* and *Tante* Adri in the bakery next door."

Here my sensibilities were slightly offended. I could see asking God to watch out for Freddy and Thea, and for *Pake* too, who was actually turning out to be rather nice at times. But *Tante* Adri!

"If it is Your will," Oma continued, "allow Freddy and Thea to come and see Linnet." Oma was quiet then and I supposed that it was my turn.

"Dear God," I said. "You are everywhere. This is what Jürgen and Willem told me, and I think this is what Oma says too. So, yes, please watch out for Freddy and Thea. Make them come here, God, so that I can see them and tell them what I have learned about You."

It was quiet again. Then I remembered what I had forgotten.

"Amen."

"That was a good prayer, Linnet."

Oma stood up. "Now I will go and make us some lunch. And while I am doing that, I want you to read the second chapter again and to make some notes or questions about things that you think are interesting or that you don't understand."

"All right, Oma."

Oma went to the kitchen and I set to reading the second chapter again. But before I had a chance to immerse myself in the sentences, there was a knock on Oma's front door. It was not very loud and, because she was in the kitchen and obviously had not heard the sound of it, I got up from the table and answered the door for her. Maybe it was *Pake*, and perhaps he needed me to deliver bread with him. But when I opened the door, a man I did not know stood on the doormat. A black hat sat on his head, a black beard flowed from his chin, and a black coat covered his small body. Surely, he was ready for hiding.

"Hello," I said, "can I help you?"

"Is *Mevrouw* Smit home?"

"Yes, I'll get her for you." I ran to the kitchen and told Oma that someone was at the door.

"Did he say who he was?"

"No, Oma."

She walked over and I trailed behind her.

"Why, *Meneer Hoffman*, how good to see you. How are you?"

Meneer Hoffman glanced behind him down the street before he spoke. "Not too well, but thank you for asking."

"Won't you step inside? It might be better for talking."

Meneer Hoffman appeared very grateful to Oma for this suggestion and, after wiping his feet thoroughly on the mat, came in rather rapidly, firmly shutting the front door behind him.

"Why don't you come and sit on the couch, *Meneer* Hoffman, and I'll make you some tea. It's very cold outside."

Oma was being most kind and gracious. *Meneer* Hoffman was short and bespectacled, giving him, I thought, a rather owlish expression. But I had never seen either a black owl or one wearing a hat. Freddy told me that owls were supposed to be wise. Was *Meneer* Hoffman wise? He followed Oma into the living room and sat down on the couch. But his black pants only touched its very edge as if he were about to leave again. Taking off his hat, he placed it next to him on the couch. It sat there like an extra person, a very quiet, sad person.

"I don't need tea, thank you for asking," *Meneer* Hoffman began. "I've actually come to tell you about our Otto. He was fired from his job yesterday. You know he worked at our newspaper?"

He stopped again, patted his hat absently and cast a furtive glance towards the window. There was no one in our lane, and I began to feel distress for the man. It was obvious that he was nervous and worried.

"I'm so sorry," Oma began, but *Meneer* Hoffman interrupted her.

"My wife and I don't know what to do. You hear so many stories about Mauthausen and Buchenwald, and we are so anxious that Otto, well, that Otto will be taken from our house by the police, by the *Gestapo*. And if they did, would they send him away?"

I wondered what Otto had done to make the police upset. Maybe Otto was a thief, or maybe he had broken someone's bicycle. Or maybe, because he worked at a newspaper, he had written something bad.

"What can I do to help you, *Meneer* Hoffman?" Oma said softly, "You are quite right. These are strange times, and stories do travel around from house to house. I have heard them as well as you."

Meneer Hoffman coughed into his hand before he continued. "There are alarming stories about all these camps, about forced transports in Germany. And my relatives in Germany . . . they write."

His black beard trembled and the eyes behind the black–rimmed glasses blinked rapidly.

"Yes, I know," Oma said soothingly, "I know. Were you thinking to send Otto away? What about yourself, *Meneer* Hoffman? What about you and your wife?"

"Oh, we are fine, Hilda and I. We are old people after all, and death is not far from us. But we worry so about the boy. He came home last night, but soldiers have constantly been walking through our street. I'm aware that they patrol all the time, but just this morning it seemed to us that they were keeping a special eye on our house."

"Do you want him to come and stay with me for a few days?"

"Oh, *Mevrouw* Smit, I didn't want to be so bold, but since you yourself are so kind as to ask, yes, that would be wonderful."

I had not understood a word of the conversation, just that Otto Hoffman had been fired from his job at the newspaper. I knew what a newspaper was, because sometimes Freddy had brought one home. I also understood that Otto was in some sort of danger. After fidgeting with his hands for a few minutes, *Meneer* Hoffman stood up.

"Maybe I can get Otto to come to you under the cover of dark, *Mevrouw* Smit, maybe this very evening I can bring him here?"

"He will be welcome, *Meneer* Hoffman," Oma replied.

"Shalom, *Mevrouw* Smit."

"Shalom, *Meneer* Hoffman."

The little black–bearded man donned his hat and almost ran to the door in his haste to leave. After the door shut behind him, Oma sat down on the couch and patted the place next to her. I came over and sat down.

"I suppose you wonder what that was all about, Linnet?"

"Yes," I affirmed.

"*Meneer* Hoffman, Linnet, is Jewish."

I sat down on the chesterfield. It was still a tiny bit warm in the spot where *Meneer* Hoffman had half-sat. Leaning my head against the back of the couch, I repeated what Oma had just said.

"*Meneer* Hoffman is Jewish?"

Oma, who had sat down as well, studied me and acknowledged my question with an inclination of her head.

"Is Thea part of his family?"

It seemed incredible to me to even consider the possibility that *Meneer* Hoffman might be related to Thea. His black beard, his black hat, his black coat and his fear – all those things did not describe my Thea at all except, of course, that she did have black hair.

"Well, yes and no," Oma responded, "It's like you and I, Linnet, we are both Dutch. We were born in this country, and we belong here in Holland. But we are not part of the same family. Your last name is Veerman and my last name is Smit. Even so, Thea is part of a race that is Jewish, just like *Meneer* Hoffman, But she is not related to him."

I didn't understand and I said so.

"Is Thea not Dutch then? She was born in Holland. She was born in Rotterdam."

"Yes, she is Dutch, Linnet. But she is also Jewish."

I conveyed by the expression on my face that I did not grasp her explanation.

"She is a Dutch Jew," Oma went on. "To be Jewish does not mean that you were born in a certain country. But it does mean that you are part of a race, part of a people who can be born in any country. You can be Jewish and born in Belgium; you can be Jewish and born in France; and you can be Jewish and born in Holland."

I sat next to Oma with a rather bewildered expression on my face.

"Jewish people," Oma continued, "have their own customs and often wear special clothes. For example, you saw *Meneer* Hoffman's black hat and black coat?"

Nodding, I said nothing, but waited for her to continue.

"Jewish people who are very serious about their faith," she added softly, "do not go to church on Sunday. They go to a building called a synagogue and they go on Saturday."

"Thea never went to the church on the island," I responded slowly, "but Freddy didn't either."

"Thea probably never took being Jewish very seriously. I think that she never considered it an important part of her life. I also think that she did not want to go to a church. Freddy probably decided to do the same thing."

"But Freddy went to church when he was little, Oma."

"Yes, he did. But I guess that he either was not taught properly, or he just plain didn't believe what he was being taught."

"Do you think that Freddy and Thea don't believe in God, Oma?"

"I don't know, child. I just don't know."

"Freddy did tell me about good and bad, Oma," I defended him, remembering what he had said about the German man. *"This man, Linnet, wants to do bad things to a great many people. He wants to take their homes away and, he also wants to ... to kill them."*

Oma merely regarded me, but she did not respond.

"Are Jewish people the people Freddy told me about on the island, the ones who had to leave their home and had no place to go?"

"Yes, I think that he probably meant the Jews, Linnet, and I
think he was probably worried that, being Jewish, Thea might be in
danger."

I could hear Freddy's voice speak to me right in Oma's living
room. *This man, Linnet, has a hunger to eat people. He has a great thirst
to swallow up countries and make himself fat by doing so. He is not a good
man and I'm afraid that there's going to be a war.*

"Why would Thea be in danger, Oma? Because she is Jewish?
Does that bad man Freddy told me about want to kill Jewish people
because they don't go to church on Sunday? I just don't understand,
Oma. This man is eating up people, Freddy said. Is that why Freddy
and Thea went away? Are they ever going to come back and be with
me?"

"You know, Linnet," Oma said quietly, "I think it's a good time
to pray again. You are very afraid and troubled. Here, fold your
hands in mine and we'll ask God to help us."

"But what if God is not true, Oma? What if Thea and Freddy
are right about not going to church?"

"Do you think they are right, Linnet?"

I leaned my head back against the couch and shut my eyes
tight. Just an hour or so ago, I had been sure, so very sure, that God
had made everything and that He was everywhere. But right now
with this new information in my heart, information that Thea could
be in danger and with the knowledge that Freddy and Thea had
probably both decided that God was probably not real – well, maybe
I should think about these matters again. They had never told me
about God, had never taken me to church, and had never read the
Bible with me. A strange loyalty brooded within my heart – a loyalty

that suggested that if I should believe in God, I would be betraying their love for me.

"I don't know, Oma, if I can pray," I answered, as I opened my eyes again, "but you can pray, because you believe for sure. Will God be mad at me if I just wait for a while before I speak with Him again?"

11

Later that evening, sitting on my cot and watching Freda scuttle busily across the floor of the attic, I wished that I could speak with Freddy and Thea; and then, after I spoke with them, I wished that I could cuddle and sit between them.

"I look forward to seeing you tomorrow, Linnet."

That's what Oma Sanne had said when I left. Had she meant it? She was probably very disappointed when I said that I wanted to wait with prayer. But how could I pray if Freddy and Thea did not pray? Not that praying itself seemed a difficult matter. If I tried to pray now, in the bedroom, then no on would be able to see that I was praying – not Freddy, not Thea, and not Oma. Of course, I always folded my hands and closed my eyes at suppertime when *Pake* said that it was time to pray. He pretty well always said the same thing before each meal, *Pake* did. *"Our great God and heavenly Father. We invoke Your blessing on this food and drink. We thank You for it. Amen."* Sometimes there was a little more. Every now and then, he prayed for the Queen. And after every meal, he said, *"For what we have received from Your hand, we thank You. Amen."* The wording at the end of each meal was occasionally phrased a little differently as well, but it all amounted to much of the same thing. If God was listening, would He be pleased to always hear *Pake* pray the same thing? Thea had always said the same thing, when she put me to bed each night – *I love you, Little Thing.* I hadn't minded that.

Freda scuttled past me again. I wished that she would come and sit in my hand or on my foot. Even if she was a mouse, she would be company, and I surely wished for a constant friend. Slowly I stood up, undressed, and put on my flannel nightgown. Thea had made it, and it was blue and warm, and that was good, because the attic was pretty cold at night now that it was winter. I put on the wool socks that Thea had knit for me too. Thea had always told me that if your feet were warm, the rest of you would warm up as well.

Oma Sanne had told me that she knelt down at the side of her bed each night to say her evening prayer. She said that she thanked God for the day and confessed her sins, although I couldn't imagine what Oma might do wrong, and then she talked to God about her problems. At the end of the prayer, she asked Him to watch over her while she slept. Without thinking, I knelt down at my cot and words tumbled out of my heart.

"You know, God," I whispered softly, my face touching the blue coverlet, "I'm sorry that I didn't talk to You at Oma's house earlier today. You see, I had just found out that Freddy and Thea probably don't talk to You. But Freddy and Thea don't talk to *Pake* and *Tante* Adri either. All the same they did have Karel bring me to live at their house. So I have to talk to *Pake* and *Tante* Adri, even though Freddy and Thea .... Well, it just seemed to me, earlier at Oma's house, that if Freddy and Thea didn't pray to You, I shouldn't pray to You either. I like to do things that they do, you see. I don't know how to explain it better. The truth is that I don't really understand. Things don't really make sense to me. But I do believe that You are real, God. This is true. But even if You are real, does that mean that I should talk to You? I wish I had a friend here, God, because I'm lonely."

Getting up, I padded over to the window on my wool socks and peeked out into the darkness. *Pake* had told me that according to a law enacted by the Germans, we should have black coverings over all our windows. Each of the windows in town had dark material hanging over them at night, but *Pake* thought my attic window was so grimy that it didn't need any covering. He didn't know that I had cleaned it up a bit. And I supposed he never thought about the skylight in the attic roof either.

I rarely switched the ceiling light bulb on. It was dirty and was an ugly light. Anyway, I usually undressed before it became very dark. There was a potty under the cot. Tante Adri had put one there so I would have no reason to go wandering about at night. Through the tiny, clear peephole in the window I could detect some movement on the sidewalk below. Though I strained to see what it was, I could make out very little. Men's voices rose up rather loudly, and I supposed some soldiers were passing by. Were they looking for Otto? *Meneer* Hoffman's son? Would there also be soldiers looking for Thea in Rotterdam? Was she hiding? If they found her, would they send her to one of the camps that *Meneer* Hoffman had mentioned?

I shuffled back to the cot, dragging my stocking feet. There was a fear in me now. I missed Freddy and Thea so much. Anxiety gnawed at my insides and turned my stomach into a sour knot. I remembered my Thea crying in bed; I recalled clearly how I had covered her with the blanket; and I could literally feel how I had kissed her cheek. Without realizing it, I knelt down in front of the cot again, my face drowning in the blue bedspread. Maybe Freddy had slept under this same bedspread.

"Father," I said, praying for the second time that night, "I'm truly sorry I didn't want to speak to you earlier with Oma. I know I said that before, but I really mean it. I have no one else to talk to right now. I don't really know You, but I need to ask You something. Please take care of Freddy and Thea in Rotterdam. Oma Sanne said "Father," so I'm saying it too, because she knows how to talk to You. Can you show me that You are real? I feel inside my heart that You are truly there. I miss Freddy and Thea so much! And . . . ."

I could not finish, because I was crying, crying so hard that I was sure the soldiers on the street, if they were still there, would hear me. My hands dropped down to the floor next to the bed, and my shoulders heaved and heaved. For a long time, there was only the sound of my sobbing, and then, when my whimpering had shrunk to an occasional sniffle, there was a tiny, cold nudge on my right hand. I froze and moved my left hand onto the bed. Gingerly turning my head and peering down towards the ground, I saw Freda's bitsy form in the semi–darkness, snuffling my right pinkie. Her little paws explored, her tiny muzzle snout was pointed downwards, her whiskers twitched and tickled my palm, and her long tail trailed behind her. Then she sat up on her hind legs and I couldn't help but begin a conversation with the little mouse, even though my nose was wet and runny and my voice quite thick.

"Hello, Freda. Have you come to see me?"

It was rather a dumb question, because there was no one there but myself.

"Would you like a raisin, Freda? They're on a little saucer on the dresser. I haven't put it down yet tonight. But if I move, will you run away?"

Freda kept on snuffling, the sound of my woebegone voice not in the least deterring her curiosity.

"You know, Freda," I went on hoarsely, "you are younger than Ko downstairs. You were made on the sixth day by God. Did you know that? Have you ever gone downstairs to visit Ko?"

Freda's pink nose quivered.

"You are nice, Freda," I continued, "and I will tell you a story. It is a fable that Freddy told me a long time ago about some mice. Are you going to stay and listen?"

Freda continued to nose the palm of my hand and did not seem intent upon leaving So I began.

"Once a upon a time . . . ." I stopped and with my left hand blew my nose into the coverlet, remembering simultaneously Oma Sanne talking to me earlier that day. *"In the beginning God. These are very important words, Linnet. I think you've heard or read fairy tales and you might remember that they often start with 'Once upon a time.'"*

Oma was right, because here I was starting a story for Freda with "Once upon a time." I cleared my throat and pondered. Freda looked up into my face. Even in the falling darkness of the room, I could see her shiny eyes.

"Well, Freda," I reiterated, "once upon a time there were some mice, just like you, but they were not happy, because a cat kept chasing them. So they all got together and wondered what they could do about the problem of the cat. Well, one of the mice, a little, smart one just like you, Freda, with a white belly, thought it would be a good idea to hang a bell around the cat's neck. That way they could hear the cat coming, and this would give them time to run away. You know, Freda," I added, "we had a cat on the island and it was Thea's idea to hang a bell around the neck of our cat. Maybe Thea got the idea from this story, what do you think?"

Freda did not comment but kept staring at me with her polished eyes, complacently seated on her hind legs. It seemed to me that she was listening with great interest. I smiled, blew my nose once more, and took up the thread of the story once more.

"You are really cute, Freda. Well, here's what happened next. All the mice thought the idea of putting a bell around the cat's neck was excellent, and they all clapped their paws. But there was one old mouse who said that although he did think it was a fine idea, he wondered who was going to volunteer to hang the bell around the cat's neck."

Freda went down on all four of her paws at this point and pattered away under the bed. I sighed.

"So you see, Freda," I called out after her, "it's great to have an idea, but it's an altogether different matter to carry it out. That's what Freddy said anyway."

I got up and took some raisins down from the dresser. Bending down, I made a little row of four raisins right next to the bed before crawling under the blankets. Tante Adri had provided a wool blanket and had tucked it under the blue coverlet. I had given her a kiss for that and she had not known what to do. Her dimples had showed but her eyes had been very surprised.

It was quite, quite dark in the attic by now. After a few minutes, I could hear a little pitter-patter, and then I sensed Freda coming out from under the bed and resuming her posture of squatting on her hind quarters next to the cot. Vaguely, I determined her outline and could see that she was beginning to gnaw away at one of the raisins.

"That's it, Freda," I whispered down to her, "eat the raisins. They came from me, you know." I watched her for a long time, and it felt good to have her crouch on the floor next to the bed. Maybe she was my friend now.

"Thank you, God," I quietly voiced up to the ceiling, "for bringing Freda when I was so sad. Is that how You are showing me that You are real? I don't know."

Both eager and anxious about going back to Oma's house the next morning, I dawdled on the sidewalk. Would she be upset with me? Would she continue to teach me from the Bible? Would she let me in the house?

I need not have worried. A few moments later, her beaming face admitted me readily into the foyer.

"Good morning, Linnet."

"Good morning, Oma."

I hung my coat on one of the pegs of the standing coat rack and walked to the living room table. Even as the day before, books covered the tablecloth. We sat down.

"We'll begin with prayer, Linnet. Now you don't have to . . . ."

"Oma, I'm sorry I said that yesterday," I whispered, my head studying the design of the tablecloth. "You see I wasn't sure if I should pray, but I thought about it last night and . . . well, I think that I should pray. I can't ask Freddy and Thea, because they are not here. But I can always ask them later."

"I am happy that you feel that way, Linnet."

Eyes crinkling with pleasure, she folded her hands. I followed her example and then we both shut our eyes.

"Dear Father," Oma began, "thank you for this beautiful day. Even though it is cold and slippery outside, we are warm and sheltered inside, and the coal in the stove is keeping us warm. Please help us as we study the Bible. Also, please keep Otto and Freddy and Thea safe and unafraid. We ask this in Jesus' name, Amen."

"Who is Jesus, Oma?"

"Yes," Oma nodded to me, "you are listening well, Linnet. Jesus is God's Son. We will talk more about Him, and who He is during our study time. Is that all right with you?"

"Yes, Oma. And can you tell me where Otto is and can I see him?"

Oma smiled.

"He is upstairs. He came last night, and his mother and father are very happy that he is here. One more thing, Linnet. I should have said this to you last night, but I didn't. That is this: You should not speak of Otto's staying here to anyone. That includes *Pake* and Tante Adri. It is really important that no one knows that Otto is here. Do you understand?"

"Yes, Oma," I answered, impressed by the way that she spoke with me, "and don't worry. I haven't said a word to anyone."

Her serious tone of voice made me feel very grown–up, very special. She trusted me, and it was as if the two of us had a secret together. And so we did. I smiled at her.

"That's my good girl!"

Oma's eyes twinkled at this juncture, and as she spoke, she walked towards the stairs – the stairs in the foyer, just across from the front door.

"Otto!"

I did not hear a reply, but soon after Oma called up, thundering footsteps crashed down the steps. Immensely curious, I dogged Oma's trail to the foyer.

"Did you call me, *Mevrouw* Smit?"

"Yes, Otto. I'd like you to meet my student and neighbor, Linnet. Linnet, this is Otto Hoffman."

"How do you do, Linnet?"

I stared at a young man who was as far from looking like his father as a periwinkle was from looking like a piece of wood. Otto was tall, brown–haired, and radiated good nature.

"Fine, thank you. How do you do, Otto?"

"Fine also. And now that this has been established, would you mind telling me what Mevrouw Smit is teaching you? You appear to me to know a great deal already."

I grinned. Otto sounded like Freddy.

"Well, Oma is teaching me adding, subtracting, Bible, and sewing. Is she teaching you anything?" I added in a very poor effort at a joke.

Otto replied, and he was most serious of a sudden, "She is teaching me thankfulness and love. And those two things, *Juffrouw* Linnet, are some of the most important things in the whole world."

I knew that he was referring to her taking him in.

"I know," I replied soberly, inadvertently glancing towards the window in the living room, a window through which the street was visible.

"Well, Otto," Oma interposed, "perhaps it's better that you stay upstairs for now, but later this morning I'll take a cup of cocoa up to you."

Otto's lips curved upward in a smile before he turned and leaped upstairs again, taking the steps two at a time. I sighed. He was nice and did so remind me of Freddy.

Back in the living room, after we sat down at the table, I expected Oma to pick up the Bible and to say that we were now at chapter three. But she didn't.

"Early this morning, Linnet, a friend of yours came by the house. I think you know him. His name is Karel."

"Karel was here?" I repeated excitedly. "Oh, yes, I know Karel, Oma! He's Freddy's friend, and he brought me here in a car when I first came. He's very kind. Was he here? Did he ask about me? Is he coming back?"

As if by magic, I suddenly heard Thea's voice. *"You are asking too many questions, Little Thing. Slow down."*

"No, he's not here any more, Linnet. But he said to say 'hello,' and that he would try to come by and see you when he could."

"Oh," I exhaled, a great big sigh escaping as I spoke. "I wish that I could have seen him, Oma. He might have told me how Freddy and Thea are."

"Well, he gave me something for you, Linnet."

"What, Oma?"

"A letter, Child."

She handed me an envelope that was lying on the table next to the Bible. My heart pounded and my hands were so eager to hold the white covering, that I clumsily dropped it onto the floor. Down I went on my hands and knees, falling onto Oma's red carpet to pick it up, banging my head on the edge of the table as I stood up.

"Oh, child!" Oma exclaimed. "Did you hurt yourself?"

"No," I answered, sitting down again.

I had never received a letter before and was now faced with the conundrum of opening it.

"Shall I help you?"

Nodding, I handed her the envelope. Oma took a knitting needle from her sewing basket and inserted the pointy end into its edge, lancing the long side open. I eagerly reached back for the white enclosure, and it took me a minute to get the letter out, my hands were so shaky. There were two pages. Holding them with my right hand, I stroked them with my left.

"Well, you best read it," Oma said rather matter–of–factly, "and while you do, I'll go and make us a cup of tea, so you can have the room all to yourself." She got up and disappeared into the kitchen.

Unfolding the pages, I placed them in front of me on the table.

"Dear Little Thing:"

The words jumped out at once and made me all warm inside. They brought tears to my eyes, and I had to wipe them before I could keep on reading.

"How we miss you, and how we long to speak with you and sit with you. It has been such a long time, and we cannot explain everything to you as clearly as we would like in a letter, but we will try. Hopefully, Karel will be able to give this letter to Oma Sanne. You see, Linnet, we did send you some messages by word of mouth through Karel, but Tante Adri, whom he saw, told him plainly that she would not pass them on. She also told him the last time that he was in town that he was not allowed to come into the shop anymore."

I stopped and stiffly leaned my head against the high backing of the chair. If I had known about Karel's visits, I might have been very angry at *Tante* Adri, but I might also have been a little less lonely. Just to know that Freddy and Thea had tried to give me a message would have helped me. Why did *Tante* Adri not tell me that Karel had been by to see me? Why had she not let him into the shop? Did *Pake* know that Karel had visited? I just did not understand *Tante* Adri. Sitting up straight, I kept on reading.

"There were many, many people killed here in Rotterdam, and about 85,000 homes were destroyed, Little Thing. Imagine that! I don't think we ever counted that high with you yet. Remember how I told you, Linnet, when we sat in the dunes that time, that a man called Hitler would try to take away homes? Well, he has done so and will continue to do so. He is not a good man."

I stroked the paper again. The soft crinkling of the parchment mingled with my labored breathing.

"There were many fires here in the big city of Rotterdam because of the bombing, and the wind prevented the fire brigade from helping too much. The middle of the city was one giant bonfire. Thea's friends lost their home and their lives."

I could again picture the little fire we would sometimes make on the beach and the shadows that danced on the sand. I recalled how we had relaxed under a huge sky twinkling with stars while waiting for the rabbits to come out. It was hard to imagine a city burning with large shadows dancing on pavement – a city much bigger than Schiermonnikoog.

"Thea was very upset. She probably caught a cold traveling from the island to the mainland. Do you recollect the trip that we made in the boat, and how chilly it was in the rain afterwards? She was able to manage for a few days, especially when she was searching and searching for her friends. But then she began coughing, and her chest hurt very badly when she breathed. Fortunately, we were close to a church that had been changed into a hospital, a place for sick people. The people in the church took us in and let me stay by her bedside. She was diagnosed with pneumonia and given medicine."

Bending my head over the paper, I saw that two tears had trickled onto it, making a wet, bluish stain. My Thea was sick, and I could not even be there to help her; I could not sit by her bedside like Freddy. Pneumonia was a frightfully long word, and for that reason it was probably very serious. I wiped my eyes and read on.

"I found a place where I could stay every night, Little Thing, and you are not to worry now as you are reading this. But now you know why we did not come back and take you to be with us. Thea is almost better, but not quite. She is very weak. Karel was to have told you all this, and he was to give you a hug from us when he came."

But he didn't see me, I thought, and there was no hug, and I did worry.

"We have some people who have offered to have both of us stay with them as soon as Thea is well enough to leave the hospital. Thea talks about

187

you every day, and she sends you a kiss and a hug. Oh, Little Thing, did you find the picture we put into your bag? We have a picture of you that Thea drew, and Thea has it next to her bed. She talks to your picture all the time, would you believe that?"

I would believe it and I smiled as I cried at the same time.

"We both hope that things are going well in the bakery. It is a very difficult time for you right now, we know that. But you are a good soldier and will learn new things each day. Pake is not a bad sort, you know. Linnet, and he can be quite kind. It's just that he cannot always bring himself to do what is right. Perhaps he didn't know that Karel was there with a message from us. Karel only saw Tante Adri."

Oma Sanne walked back into the living room with some tea. She set a cup and saucer down in front of me on the table. Then she returned to the kitchen to fetch another plate with my favorite *koek*. I remembered that Freddy had often eaten treats here. I wished I could serve him a piece of *koek* at this very moment. Maybe he and Thea would be able to come for me soon.

I put my finger under the sentence I had read last. There were not a great many sentences left in the letter. I didn't really want to read on to where there would be no more lines at all, to where it would say, "Well, Little Thing, I have to go now." As long as there were more lines and words, there was an almost physical bond.

"Well, dear Linnet . . . ."

You see, there it was. Oma had taken her place next to me. She said nothing, but just leaned back in her chair.

"Well, dear Linnet, the time has come for me to finish this letter to you. We love you so very much and wish we could see you. We will try to come as soon as we can, dear Little Thing. We really will try. But Thea has to be a bit better before we can leave Rotterdam, and I dare not leave her alone. So for now, you will have to make the best of it. And knowing your courage and sweetness, I trust you will be all right. Your very loving Freddy and Thea."

I sat up straight and once more stroked the pages. They lay on the table with several dark blots on them from where my tears had landed. Oma reached out her hand and put it on my lap.

"Are you all right, Linnet?"

I shook my head. "No."

"Would you like to tell me what the letter said?"

"You may read it, Oma," I answered, my voice thick with tears, "if you want to."

Taking her hand off my lap, she put on her gold–rimmed glasses before picking up the pages. I watched as she scanned the words, watched her face for any emotion she might show. But her face registered no feeling until the second page when she tut–tutted a bit. Then she folded the letter neatly and tucked it back into the envelope.

"It's a good thing," she then began, "that Karel was able to come here this morning, don't you think?"

"Yes."

"It's wonderful too, isn't it, Child," she went on, "that Thea is recovering from pneumonia. Do you know what pneumonia is, Linnet?"

I shook my head.

"Well, it is a sickness that begins with a cough, and that cough might worsen with a pain in the chest. There is often fever and much tiredness. But they have medicine which helps pneumonia go away, and isn't it a good thing that Thea is getting that medicine?"

"Yes."

"And how amazing is it that Freddy can nurse Thea for you and sit by her bedside every day. I would venture to think that he is a very capable nurse, wouldn't you say so?"

"Oma," I said softly, "are you trying to make me feel better?"

She smiled and replied, "Yes, of course I am. It's always good to count your blessings, Child. God gives us blessings every day. We have to remember them before we can count them. And that was three blessings there, right in a row."

"Yes," I agreed, and then went on to ask, "Do you think that Karel will come back soon?"

"Well," Oma hesitated before she answered, "I don't know, Linnet. I do know he will keep his word. But he is very busy. He brought you here and he is doubtless bringing others to safe places as well."

"What do you mean, Oma?"

Oma grimaced, "That is probably something I shouldn't have said, Linnet. Nowadays it seems to be wiser to keep your mouth shut rather than open. Sometimes the less you know the better."

"Should I tell *Pake* that I got a letter from Freddy and Thea?"

"I wouldn't do that, Linnet. *Tante* Adri is bound to hear of it if you tell him, and she might make it difficult for you."

190

"Why, Oma?"

She shrugged.

"I don't know how the hearts and minds of some people work, Linnet. Perhaps, in some strange way, she was happy to see Freddy leave so many years ago, so that she could have *Pake* all to herself. But that's enough talk now. It's time to do some reading and other work."

It was chapter three of Genesis which we read out loud together. Then Oma told me, as she had told me with Chapter Two, to read it again and to answer questions as best I could, questions that she had written down on a piece of paper. Leaving me to work, Oma went upstairs with a cup of cocoa for Otto.

The questions were: How did Adam and Eve disobey? Did they know that they had done something wrong? Did God punish the snake? Did God punish Adam and Eve for disobeying?

I read the chapter again. Then I leaned back and tried to think. Most of the time, my attention wandered. It wandered away from the questions and back to the letter, and my hands inadvertently stole over to the top of the tablecloth and stroked the envelope again and again. How did Adam and Eve disobey? Well, I wrote down, they ate the fruit of the one tree that God had told them not to eat from. Did they know they had done wrong? I usually knew when I had done wrong. I caressed the letter and memories flooded over me.

Once, Thea had made me two dresses – one for special days and one for ordinary days. The special one was pink, had a lace collar and a butterfly pocket. The everyday one was blue, but it had no pockets. One ordinary day, I had put on the dress for special days after lunch. It was a day when Thea was feeling creative and was out doing some painting in the dunes. Wearing the special dress, I had sneaked out the back door to go for a walk with Freddy.

When I came outside, prancing before him in my finery, he had said, "Little Thing, that's an exceptionally pretty dress to wear on a walk, isn't it?"

"Yes," I had answered, "but it's such a special and very pretty day, isn't it?"

He had grinned, shrugged, and off we went birdwatching. Coming home later that afternoon through a farmer's field, we encountered a barbed wire fence.

"Well, Linnet," Freddy declared, "here's a problem. If we want to be home by suppertime and not have Thea angry, we have to be adventurous. So hold on, I'm lifting you high and right over top of this obstacle."

So he had lifted me high into the sky and had swung me over the fence. But my skirt ballooned out and the beautiful pink material caught on the barbs, and a tear, an enormous tear that could not be fixed by Freddy, showed up below my knees. The tear shouted out that I was in big trouble. It would not be Freddy's trouble. Freddy didn't know that the special dress I was wearing had been off limits; he didn't know that I had been instructed not to wear it on ordinary days.

Did I know that I had done wrong? Yes, I surely did. Had I wanted to hide like Adam and Eve hid? Yes, I wanted totally to disappear, and when we came home, I had tried to do just that by hiding in the privy. But Thea had called.

"Where are you, Linnet?"

Oma's living room swam back into my view and I wrote into the notebook that Oma had given me: "Yes, they knew they had done wrong." The next question was, "Did God punish the snake?" Well, the snake had to go on his belly and eat dust. Maybe he had eaten other things before that; and perhaps he had been able to walk or fly. He would have made a very skinny bird. But truthfully, I had never heard of a snake with wings. Actually, I had never really seen a snake at all except on pictures. But the answer was, and I wrote it down in my notebook, "Yes, God did punish the snake."

The last question read: "Did God punish Adam and Eve for disobeying?" Well, yes, He did, and this is what I wrote down. There was quite a bit in the chapter that I did not understand, and there were words that I did not comprehend. I fingered the letter again. Had Freddy and Thea ever read Genesis? I heard Oma coming down the stairs, and I bent my head over the Bible to show her that I was working hard.

"Well, Linnet," she said as she walked into the living room, "how are your questions coming?"

"I don't understand everything, Oma," I confessed, "but I answered the questions."

"Yes, I didn't think you would understand everything. So let's talk about it."

Oma sat down next to me. "Stop me, Linnet, if I say something that is not clear. But I will review what we have read so far as a story."

I nodded and she began.

"In the beginning, after He had created the heavens and the earth, God made two people. Their names were Adam and Eve, and they were perfect. They were beautiful to look at, and what they did and said was without any mistakes. God loved Adam and Eve. He let them live in a splendid, lovely garden called Eden. He told them to take care of everything – of the land animals, of the birds, and all the fish, and all of nature around them. It was a wonderful job that He gave them. There were no weeds in the garden. The animals were friendly, and the birds that you love so, Linnet, sang the most melodious, the most sweet-sounding songs you have ever heard. And there was no death. Adam and Eve were very happy. How could they not be, living in such an amazing garden?

"And there was only one command that God gave Adam and Eve. Do you remember what it was, Linnet?"

"Yes," I eagerly contributed, "they could not eat of the one tree in the middle of the garden."

"Good!" Oma praised and went on. "One day, the snake came over to Adam and Eve. He singled out Eve and told her to look at the fruit of the tree. He tempted her by saying: 'Doesn't that look delicious, Eve?' When Eve saw that the fruit seemed good, she coveted it, that is to say, her mouth began to water. Then the snake lied to Eve. He told her that God had not really said that they couldn't eat the fruit; that they would not really die as God had said; and that, if they did eat of the fruit, she and Adam would be like God. Eve wanted to believe him. She wanted to eat the fruit very badly.

"So, although Eve knew she shouldn't, she ate. She also gave some of the fruit to Adam who was with her, and he ate too. As soon as they had swallowed the forbidden fruit, they knew that they had done wrong. The wrong enveloped them; it embraced them inside and out; and they felt dirty. Although they covered themselves with leaves to hide this dirty feeling, the covering didn't help them feel any cleaner. Stripped of the beauty and goodness with which God had created them, they knew they were now dirty and undressed, and they hid when they heard God coming. Why do you think they hid, Linnet?"

"Because they did wrong and were scared?"

"Yes, because they did wrong and were scared. You see God is perfect. There is no wrong in Him anywhere. He can't abide anything wrong. Adam and Eve knew they could not stand in front of Him any longer, because they had done wrong, and they knew they could not walk in the garden with Him any longer, because they had done wrong. They were no longer clean. They had sinned. Sin is a word for wrong, Linnet.

"Then God called out to Adam and Eve. What did He say, Linnet?

"He said, 'Where are you?'"

"Good!" Oma praised again. "That's good remembering, Linnet."

It was quiet for a bit, except for the ticking of the clock. I glanced at Oma. She was frowning as if in deep thought. "Don't you remember the rest, Oma?" I asked. "We can read it again if you like."

"No, I do remember," she said, "but I want to say it in the right way so that you will understand." A few moments later she continued. "Were you surprised when you heard a snake talking in the story, Linnet?"

"No, Oma. Freddy often tells me stories with animals talking."

"Who do you think the snake is?"

"I don't know, but I don't like him at all. He lied."

"Yes, and actually that's one of his names, Linnet. The snake has more than one name. One of these is the Father of all lies. He is also called the serpent, or Satan, or the devil. He hates God and wants everyone else to hate him too."

"Why?"

"You are a why person, aren't you, Linnet? The answer to that why question I can't give properly. I can only tell you that Satan, before he showed up in the garden, was an angel. An angel is a being who lives with God in His home in heaven. God has many angels. They are messengers and do what He asks. Well, Satan was one of these angels. But he was proud and jealous and he wanted to be like God. So God threw Satan out of heaven along with some other bad angels. Since that time, Satan and his followers have been at war with God, and he is the most wicked being alive."

"Freddy says Hitler, the man who is making war, is a very bad person. Is he Satan?"

"No, but I do believe he is one of Satan's servants."

"Oh."

"Now back to Adam and Eve. They did confess to God that they did what Satan had told them to do; that they ate of the fruit that God had told them not to eat. It was good of them to own up to that. When we do something wrong, God wants us to say that we sinned, that we did wrong, and that we are sorry. The moment we do so, He becomes our Helper."

Oma stopped again, but only for a moment. Her hands lay in her lap. Maybe her oma had taught her all these things, and she had sat at a table and learned them, just as I was learning them.

"The devil, or Satan, was punished by God, Linnet," she went on. "Do you remember how?"

"Yes, he had to go on his belly and eat dust. I was on my belly when we were hiding from the German soldier, Oma. Only I had sand in my mouth."

Smiling at me, Oma went on, "Yes, I remember that you told me that. Now earlier you asked, 'Who is Jesus?' And I told you that He is God's Son. Verse 14 talks about Jesus, Linnet. Just read it for me."

So I read: *"I will put enmity between you and the woman, between your seed and her seed; He shall bruise your head and you shall bruise His heel."*

The text was gibberish to me. I did not understand the words at all, and it showed on my face.

"I know," Oma said, "it's a difficult verse. Let me help you a little bit. First of all, "enmity" means "hatred," and "seed" means "children." God is saying that He will put hatred between the snake's children and Eve's children."

"So, the snake's children and Eve's children don't get along," I asserted.

"That is right, Linnet. From this time on, there would be two kinds of people – those who would listen to Satan, and those who would listen to God."

"Is that so today too, Oma?"

"Yes, Linnet. A person is either a child of God, or he is a child of the devil."

"Are you a child of God, Oma?"

She nodded and I went on.

"Is *Pake* one?"

"I hope so, Linnet."

"Am I a child of God, Oma?"

"I hope so, Linnet."

There were an awful lot of things to think about. My head was full of thoughts.

Oma went on. "In time, a baby would be born. The baby's name would be Jesus."

"So Eve was going to have a baby called Jesus?"

"Well, yes and no. Eve would have many children, and her children would have children, and these children would have children too. Many, many years later, a girl called Mary became the mother of Jesus. Jesus was born to save us. He was born to bring us back to God. He was born so we could walk with Him again."

It was quiet again, and in the quiet I thought that I most certainly did not want to be a child of the devil. I put my hand on my belly. Imagine crawling on your belly all day long and eating dust. Oma cleared her throat and was about to go on when there was a knock at the door. She got up, gave me a pat on the head in passing, and walked into the foyer. When she opened the door, I could hear *Pake's* voice.

"I'm sorry to disturb you, *Mevrouw* Smit, but I have some extra deliveries to make yet this morning and early this afternoon. Adri has a headache, and an order just came in. It would be most helpful for me to have Linnet along. She can come back tomorrow."

"Linnet," Oma called out over her shoulder, "*Pake* is here." But I had heard his words and was already putting on my coat.

"I'm coming, *Pake.*"

12

ake owned a large delivery bicycle. It had a big carrier in front of the steering wheel, and in it he could transport many of loaves of his bread, many packages of his raisin buns, and many carefully wrapped cakes. He had a regular clientele who expected him to bring them certain items each week, but sometimes extra orders arrived. When I walked out of Oma's house, buttoning my coat as I did so, he was waiting by the side of the road in front of the shop, his carrier loaded to the brim.

"Hop on, Linnet," he called out, "and we'll be off."

Running over, I jumped up onto the back seat of the bicycle and put my arms around his waist. *Pake* pushed off immediately and began peddling. It was chilly out, and I hugged his overcoat for warmth. I loved riding on the bike over the main street's cobblestones. Sometimes I opened my mouth and made an "aah" sound. The noise converted into a pleasing, bumpy, musical note, reverberating deep down in my throat.

At other times, I sang a song, and once or twice, *Pake* had joined in. The last time he had joined in was when I had burst into a patriotic rendition of the Dutch national anthem, the *Wilhelmus* song. Freddy had told me that it had been written almost four hundred years ago, and that this made it one of the oldest national anthems in the world. I only knew the first verse, and now, moved by my eventful morning, I began to carol it rather loudly past *Pake's* tweed coat.

Wilhelmus van Nassouwe, ben ik van Duitsen bloed..
Den Vaderland getrouwe, blijf ik tot in den dood.
Een Prinse van Oranje, ben ik, vrij onverveerd,
Den Koning van Hispanje, heb ik altijd geèrt.

As I had hoped, *Pake* joined in. His rather weak tenor grew louder as we turned the corner onto the main street, and I hugged the rough, tweed fabric of his coat, singing into its warmth. We passed the church just as we were on the last line of the song. *Pake* stopped peddling, and we halted in front of a red–bricked, two-story house. I knew that the minister and his family lived here. Sliding down from the back seat, I walked to the front carrier and looked questioningly at *Pake*.

"Four loaves, Linnet," he directed, "and mind you that *Mevrouw* Prins pays. That's thirty–two cents, girl, and don't let her pull one over on you."

"Yes, *Pake*," I answered, carefully extracting the bread from the carrier.

Dandling the four loaves in my arms as if they were babies, I advanced up the path towards the door. It opened wide before I got there, and *Mevrouw* Prins, tall and blond, stood in the doorway.

"Hello, Linnet," she greeted, "and have you brought us our bread?"

"Yes, *Mevrouw* Prins," I answered, handing the loaves to her, "here they are. And *Pake* says it's thirty–two cents, please."

She put the bread on the hall table stationed next to the door before turning back to me and waving at *Pake*. "Didn't I pay extra last time?" she pondered, as she commenced to contemplating the sky which was dark with rain.

"No, *Mevrouw* Prins," I disagreed politely, staring up at the sky as well. "I don't think so."

"Well," she frowned, "I suppose I must bring out my wallet then and pay, mustn't I?"

Reaching down into her apron pocket, she produced a *porte-monnaie*, a small and dilapidated, brown leather purse. Zipping it open, she shook out some change into her hand. Counting slowly and carefully, at length the desired amount fell into my outstretched hand.

"There you are then, Linnet."

"Thank you, *Mevrouw*."

I turned and ran back to *Pake*, gave him the money, and he winked at me just before I hopped back onto the bike.

"Good girl, Linnet."

We made eight more deliveries in and around town, and just as I thought we were heading home, *Pake* turned the steering wheel sharply to the right and drove onto the grass path leading towards the park by the river. It was a hobbly, rather rough and uneven ride. I hung on tightly.

"Where are we going, *Pake*?"

My voice joggled as we swerved on the curving path. Even as we headed towards the river, I could see a group of eight soldiers out of the corner of my eye, walking two-by-two right past our small street. *Pake* didn't answer my question, but peddled as far as he could down the small trail leading to the water. Some ducks preened on the grass, while others lay sleeping, and I was sorry I didn't have any bread crumbs with me.

"Ducks have very good eyesight, Little Thing. They will never need glasses."

I grinned to myself. Freddy sure knew a lot. When *Pake* had bread to spare in the bakery, he often let me go and feed the ducks, and I loved doing that. I bounced off the back seat before *Pake* stopped the bike. He got off slowly, precariously leaning the vehicle against a bush. It was getting chillier out, and I was also getting hungry and hoped that *Tante* Adri's headache would not prevent her from making us a late lunch.

"Linnet," *Pake* said, "I've brought you here to . . . ." He stopped, stopped so long that I became uneasy. Was he going to tell me something bad about Freddy? Had something happened to him? or to Thea?

"What, *Pake*?"

Three ducks waddled up to us and quacked. They were questioning quacks. The hens knew me because of my frequent feedings and were expecting some snippets of bread. *Pake* was staring at the water as if he hoped the ripples would help him formulate words.

"*Pake*?"

The New Has Come

He turned towards me and I was horrified to see tears in his eyes.

"Did something awful happen to Freddy, *Pake*," I whispered.

"No, child," he answered and turned so that I could not see his face anymore.

"What then?"

"I want to tell you, Linnet" he continued, still facing away from me, "that *Tante* Adri saw young Otto Hoffman go into *Mevrouw* Smit's place last night. As you might already know," he went on with apparent great difficulty, repeating himself, "as you might already know, *Tante* Adri does not like Jewish people."

"Why, *Pake*?"

There, I had said it. I had finally posed the question that had bothered me for such a long time.

"Because when she was a little girl, there was an incident at her grade school."

"An incident?"

"Something unpleasant happened to her. She and Mies, your *Beppe*, were in grade three, I think. The teacher, a *Juffrouw* Roos, was instructing the class in longhand script, and *Tante* Adri found this hard."

I nodded. This I could fully understand. Thea had started to teach me cursive writing, but I was very slow at adapting to this skill. Not being allowed to lift the pen from the paper when you were writing was not easy. *Pake* shifted his posture, and now he was staring me full in the face.

"*Tante* Adri was left-handed," *Pake* went on, "and Miss Roos was of the opinion that her students should use their right hand when they were writing. Every time *Tante* Adri unintentionally used the wrong hand, the teacher would slap her left palm with her wooden ruler."

"Oh."

It was a sympathetic "oh." I could not imagine Thea ever hitting me with anything, certainly not with a wooden ruler. If I couldn't manage to do something, Thea always sat down, put her arm about me, and said, *"Now, Little Thing, let's just try that again."*

"That wasn't all," *Pake* proceeded with his story, *"Juffrouw* Roos also humiliated *Tante* Adri many times because she was . . . well, Tante Adri was a little overweight at that time already. She was a plump child, and the teacher singled her out and called her a spoiled, overfed, and lazy student."

"I'm sorry for *Tante* Adri, *Pake*," I said, contemplating a fat duck as it doddered towards the water, probably to do some dabbling. Dabbling ducks, Freddy had taught me, had tiny rows of plates inside their beaks. These plates were called lamellae. *"Very good, Little Thing."* Freddy would have liked feeding the ducks with me. Maybe he had fed ducks here a long time ago. *Tante* Adri was not fond of the ducks. Poor Tante Adri!

I looked at *Pake* and said, "That teacher was not very nice to Tante Adri."

You could never tell a duck that he was overfed or lazy, because ducks were always chubby. Ducks just ate, and when they ate in the water, they stuck their tails into the air and stretched their heads into the water to reach their food. Tante Adri was not a duck, but she did eat a lot. And I had yet to see her eat a slice of bread with contentment.

"You are right, Linnet. *Tante* Adri's teacher was not very nice," *Pake* interrupted my thoughts, "and the teacher was Jewish. *Tante*

Adri has never been able either to forgive or to forget that year at school, and that is why she has an extreme hatred of anything and everything Jewish."

"Oh," I pondered out loud, trying to absorb the information, "but you don't hate Jewish people, do you, *Pake*?"

Pake turned and intently bored his eyes into mine. It was as if he were saying, "How could you even think such a thing of me?" After a few seconds, he shrugged.

"No, I don't hate Jewish people, but at the time of Freddy's marriage, I went along with *Tante* Adri, and I am sorry that I did."

"When you are sorry," I responded immediately, still full of the words Oma Sanne had given me earlier that morning, "and you tell God that you have done wrong, then He becomes your Helper."

Pake now focused on me in a most peculiar way. Then, turning away, he began to study the water. Two of the ducks were now swimming very close to where we were standing. Their webbed feet were like paddles. Freddy had told me that duck's feet never got cold, because the warm blood from their body went right into their feet. My toes were getting cold. *Pake* turned back to me. His blue eyes appeared determined and rather fierce.

"When we get back home, I want you to go to Oma Sanne's house right away, Linnet," he said emphatically, "and I want you to tell her that *Tante* Adri went to the *Grüne Polizei*, the Green Police, this morning to report on what she saw. I want you to relate to her that *Tante* Adri told the police that a Jewish student who was fired from a Jewish newspaper is hiding in her house."

A red alert went on in my brain. Oma Sanne had warned me not to speak of Otto at all. *Pake* was checking out the reaction on my face. I looked away. Everything he had said was true, right down to Otto's name. Otto had been working for a newspaper and he had been fired. So I took a chance. *Pake* had said that he was sorry, and he seemed sincere. Turning, I established contact with his eyes again.

"Otto hasn't done anything wrong, *Pake!*" I blurted out, thereby admitting that what he had said was true.

"I know. But the German police, like *Tante* Adri, don't care for Jews. In any case, they told her that they would send some of their men to search *Mevrouw* Smit's home tonight."

"How . . . ?" I began and stopped.

Pake went on. "Linnet, as I said before, I want you to go to Oma Sanne's house as soon as we arrive back home. I want you to take that student and bring him into our shop. I will make sure that *Tante* Adri is upstairs and resting. Look out of *Mevrouw* Smit's front window, and when you see me sweeping the sidewalk, then you'll know that the coast is clear. We'll bring the student up to your bedroom, and he can stay there tonight."

With that, *Pake* did an about-face and walked back quickly to the bush where his bicycle half-dangled, half-stood. I followed at a slower pace, one foot in front of the other, inadvertently picking up and beginning to perform the goose step. Was I to believe him?

"*Pake*?"

Hands on the steering wheel, he faced at me.

"*Pake*, did Freddy ever read Genesis with you?"

He lifted his eyebrows in a quizzical way.

"I just wondered," I persisted, "if you told him about the snake. You know, the snake who is the father of lies."

I don't quite know why those words came out of my mouth at that time. Perhaps because I wanted *Pake* to confirm in some way that what he was telling me was truthful and would turn out for the good. He neither responded nor mounted his bike, but walked the length of the little trail back to the road quietly. Even at the road, he did not get back on his bike, but kept on walking towards our lane.

The milkman passed us with his wagon, just before we got to the shop. *Pake* waited until the vehicle had juddered by on the rough lane before he spoke again. But he did not look at me directly.

"Linnet, did you clearly understand what I just told you?"

"Yes, *Pake*."

"Well, then it's all settled."

I sprinted to Oma Sanne's, and my stomach hoped that maybe she would give me some tea and a piece of koek. And I also hoped that she would know just what to do.

It took a little while for me to explain to Oma what *Pake* had just told me. A frown clouded her forehead. She appeared distressed and then called Otto to come downstairs. He came quickly, and Oma repeated the story to him, telling him he'd have to pack up and go with me later that afternoon. I could tell Otto was a little concerned too, because he kept glancing towards the window as Oma spoke.

"Don't worry, Otto," I encouraged, "I'm on the third floor, right at the top, and there's a closet in my room, and there's also a space under my bed where you can hide."

He laughed nervously and reached his right hand up to stroke his chin. It was stubbly. The sprouting of a few hairs suggested the beginnings of a small beard.

"I'll pack some sandwiches," Oma said, "because you're apt to get hungry tonight."

"My mouse, Freda, will be your friend if you feed her some bread crumbs," I informed him, trying to make the situation more agreeable.

Otto took very little notice of what I said. He was studying the empty street in earnestness. When Oma came back with a brown paper bag, he did not even turn to look at her when he spoke.

"Please tell my parents what has happened."

"Yes," Oma answered, "we surely will do that."

"No," Otto changed his mind, "maybe it's better that they don't know. They would only worry."

The clock ticked. I went over and stood by Otto. After all, I did have to keep an eye out for when *Pake* decided to sweep the sidewalk. At the same time, I wished with all my heart that Oma would make me a brown paper bag with some food in it as well.

"What if the police come to search before the evening?' Otto submitted.

"Then you will go out the back door and hide in the Veerman's shed until they are gone."

Oma had obviously been thinking, and I applauded her in my mind. She was smart, almost as smart as Freddy. I was about to tell her that, but she disappeared back into the kitchen. Would Freddy and Thea be hiding like Otto? I slipped my hand into Otto's and squeezed it.

Smiling down at me, he winked. "Well, Linnet, it looks like you and I will be well acquainted before all this is over."

"Don't worry," I said, "there are lots of people helping you. And *Tante* Adri will never imagine that you are in the attic with me."

Oma Sanne returned to the living room carrying a tray. It held some wonderful things – pieces of *koek*, hot steaming cups of cocoa, and some little pieces of cheese. My stomach rumbled louder than the clock ticked.

"Oh, you poor Child," Oma called out. "You must be starving. Come and sit down at the table with me and have a bite to eat."

I let go of Otto's hand and was only too happy to oblige.

It was well nigh just after three o'clock when we finally sighted *Pake* emerging from the shop, a broom in his hand. He began to sweep most purposefully. Dust was airborne and settling on the hard-packed dirt lane.

"I guess that means he's ready," I said. "Are you ready, Otto?"

"Yes," he answered. "I'm about as ready as I'll ever be. Goodbye, *Mevrouw* Smit. Thank you for putting up with me."

He offered her his hand, but Oma hugged Otto and kissed him on his stubbly chin and cheek. "You better go now," she advised, "but should things go wrong, you can always come back after they search here."

"Well, I'm not sure that would be wise," Otto replied. "It might put you in danger too. Besides, I'm sure they'll keep watching your house for awhile."

I was attending the window while they were saying goodbye, and to my horror saw six soldiers approaching *Pake* while he swept the sidewalk. He stopped his work as the little troop marched past him, even saluting them with his broom. The soldiers continued at a slower pace as they neared our house. But even though Otto was now at the back door, there was no need to worry. All six of the uniformed men did not even so much as glance in the direction of our window. They only stared straight ahead. Moving their black boots in unison, they carried on, and once more I marveled that their steps were so incredibly aligned.

"It's all right, Otto," I whisper-called, "they've passed and didn't even bother to look at our house. We'll wait until they're totally gone, and then you can come with me to the bakery."

Otto joined me at the window, considering the retreating green backs. I stood by him, but then noted another disconcerting fact. *Pake* had disappeared inside. Was there a reason for that? Had *Tante* Adri woken? When I mentioned it to Oma Sanne, she frowned. But a minute later, the bakery door reopened, and *Pake* resurfaced, broom in hand. We speculated that the coast must now be clear. But just as I was about to suggest that we go and walk towards the bakery, the back door opened and Karel walked in.

"Hello," he said, and I flew into his arms. He lifted me off the floor and swung me high into the air before setting me down again.

"Oh, Karel," I sang out, "I'm so glad to see you."

"And I you, Poppet," he replied. "And much as I would like to discuss my missing you, I'm afraid that I'm rather in a hurry."

"In a hurry?" I repeated, not understanding.

"Yes, Poppet. I'm here to pick up your friend, Otto. He's to come with me and come at once, for I understand that there has been some foul play going on over here with some people in this neck of the woods blabbing to the Green Police."

Oma sat down at the table and looked rather bewildered, as bewildered as I felt inside.

"I'll tell you what you ought to know rather quickly," Karel said quietly. "Just be informed that the *Grüne Polizei* are after you, Otto, for writing some article which apparently does not make the Germans out to be as fine and upstanding as they would like to appear."

We were all quiet, digesting what Karel had said. He went on, talking rapidly.

"I've got a car waiting a few streets over, and I've been told to get you to the car and to drive you out of here as fast as I can."

"But *Pake* . . . ," I ventured, thinking of him sweeping the sidewalk and now probably waiting inside the bakery for me to show up with Otto.

"Yes, *Pake*," Karel repeated, "and I don't know what to make of the man. You be very careful, Poppet. By the way, Freddy and Thea send their love, and right now, I'm to give you a big hug from both of them.

I received his hug gladly. Indeed, I could feel Freddy and Thea's love as Karel's big arms enfolded me.

"I know this is hard to understand, Poppet," he whispered, "and I hope it turns out all right in the long run. But truly, we've got to skedaddle, me and Otto."

He stood up, shook Oma Sanne's hand, and then he and Otto were out the back door before we had time to say or ask anything else. We watched them, Oma and I, from the back door. They raced across the small lawn, climbed the neighbor's fence, and disappeared into a fast encroaching mist.

"Well, Linnet," Oma said, "now we better think about what you should say to *Pake*."

"Should I tell him what happened?"

"No, I don't think so," Oma thoughtfully debated, "but I haven't any idea yet as to what you should say."

The clock struck the half hour. I sat down on the couch. Perhaps by this time Karel and Otto were driving out of town. Oma sat down next to me.

"We should pray for their safety, Linnet," she suggested, "What do you think?"

I nodded and we both folded our hands.

"Dear Father in heaven," Oma began. "We want to praise your name for your continued goodness to us. Thank you that we may always come to you and speak with you. We just want to ask you, Father, to take care of Karel and Otto. Keep them safe, and bring Otto to a place where he will be protected from the Germans. Also, Lord, keep Freddy and Thea safe, and let it be that Thea will soon be better. For Jesus' sake, Amen."

We sat quietly for a moment, our hands still folded. The clock ticked, and I wondered if *Pake* would be angry if I did not come back to the bakery soon.

"I have it, Linnet," Oma suddenly exclaimed, startling me. "You are to say that Otto went away on his own. That when you noticed *Pake* sweeping outside the shop the second time and went to get Otto, he was gone. That we, you and I, looked for him everywhere, but that he had disappeared, that all his things were gone, and that we had no idea at all where he went."

I stared at her. "But Oma Sanne, wouldn't that be lying?"

"Yes, I suppose so, Linnet."

"Is that all right to do sometimes – to lie?"

I could see myself standing in the little park speaking with *Pake*, asking him if Freddy had ever read Genesis with him, wanting to know if he knew about the snake, the father of lies. Oma answered my question.

"Lying is wrong, but strangely enough, it is sometimes necessary to save lives. Telling *Pake*, and this would probably mean telling *Tante* Adri too, that what just happened here with Otto could possibly mean that the German police might try to follow Karel and Otto. If the police caught up with them, this would mean imprisonment for both of the men."

I understood to some degree and tried to grasp it hard with my mind. Oma went on. "Lying is truly a sin, but God, I believe, will hold the Germans responsible for that sin."

I nodded.

"The blame for the lie," Oma Sanne continued slowly, while adjusting the glasses on her nose, "will fall squarely on the shoulders of those who made it necessary."

"Well," I contributed slowly, "I will tell *Pake* that Otto went away, and that I do not know where he went. That much is true."

"Yes, Child," Oma sighed. "Just remember that someone who wants information for the purpose of evil, that person has no right to the truth. He has turned his back on the truth and is himself a follower of the Father of Lies."

I did understand that.

13

When I opened the door to the bakery not too much later, *Pake* was helping a customer at the counter. *Tante* Adri was nowhere to be seen. It was nice and warm in the shop, and I smelled the fresh aroma of cookies and bread appreciatively.

"Hello, Linnet," *Pake* said.

"Hello, *Pake.*"

I was a little taken aback by the fact that he had a customer. Suppose that Otto had come into the shop with me, then the customer would have seen Otto. But what of that? And how could *Pake* stop a customer from coming in? Besides that, what were the chances that the customer would know Otto, would know that he was running away from the police? But in this town a lot of people knew one another.

I walked through the shop and waited in the hallway until the store was empty. Then I stepped back in.

"Where is the student?" *Pake* was wiping the counter with his white apron as he spoke.

"He is gone, *Pake*."

"Gone?"

"Yes, gone. After you came out the second time with the broom and began sweeping again, I was ready to get him. But when Oma and I called up to him that it was time to leave, he did not come down. So we went upstairs to see where he was, but we couldn't find him. His clothes were gone, his suitcase was gone, his books were gone, and we don't know where he went. We searched everywhere, but . . . ."

I stopped abruptly, not knowing what else I should say. *Pake* still stood by the counter, holding his apron up in mid-air as if he were about to wipe the counter once again. But he was just standing there, not wiping at all.

"What did *Mevrouw* Smit think?" he asked a moment later.

"Well, she didn't know where he had gone either. So we sat down on the couch, *Pake*, Oma and I, and we prayed for his safety."

Surely it was all right to say that to *Pake*. Surely praying was a thing that did not need to be hidden.

"Well," *Pake* responded, "I guess we can't do anything about that."

"No, *Pake*," I agreed.

He seemed lost in thought, and I greatly desired the privacy of my attic bedroom, so that I could also think, so that I could sit and quietly mull over what had happened. *Pake* paid no more attention to me at all, but disappeared into the side baking room. Turning into the hallway, I began my climb up, taking great care to avoid the creaky eighth step. The last thing in the world I wanted was to waken *Tante* Adri.

But as I tiptoed down the hall towards the second set of stairs, her voice startled me.

"Linnet?"

Somewhat gravelly in tone, it crawled out like an insect from under the bedroom door. I stiffened, stopping dead in my tracks. How could she possibly have heard me? I had been so very quiet.

"Yes, *Tante* Adri?"

"Can you come in here for a moment, Linnet?"

I opened the door to the bedroom a tiny crack, just as I had done that day when I had told Ko that I was going to visit Oma Sanne. *Tante* Adri was lying on the bed, seemingly washed out. Ko sat on his perch and blinked at me, as if to say, *Be careful, girl! Be very careful!*

"I'm sorry I didn't see you today, Linnet. It was good of you to go with *Pake* and do the deliveries. We put a '*Closed*' sign on the shop while you were gone."

"Oh, I didn't mind helping," I answered dutifully, and truly I hadn't minded.

"Well, he appreciated your help."

Ko chirped and I smiled at him.

"So, how did your time with *Mevrouw* Smit go today?"

That was an innocent question, or was it? I hesitated before I spoke.

"It went fine, *Tante* Adri. We're just starting to talk about Jesus. About who He is."

"I see."

"Do you know who Jesus is, *Tante* Adri?"

I truly don't know why I asked her that. She very likely knew the answers to all the Bible questions.

"Of course, I do, you silly child. Everyone knows who Jesus is."

"Oma Sanne is teaching me a lot of things, Tante Adri."

Tante Adri's voice, which had been irritable, now softened right down.

"What else did she teach you today, Linnet? What else did you and *Mevrouw* Smit study and do together?"

Because this was the very first time that *Tante* Adri had expressed any interest in what I was learning, I became very cautious. Did she want me to tell her that during my studies I had met Otto? Did she want to know if the police had come to Oma's house to arrest him? Did she want to know if they had taken him away? Surely it would be safe to tell her about schoolwork.

"Well," I responded slowly, "we haven't really gotten into long-hand writing or into adding and subtracting yet, but I think we will. We were just doing Bible study when *Pake* came to the door to ask if I could help out. Tomorrow we will probably do a lot more writing and adding and subtracting. Would you like me to bring my notebooks home so that you can see them, *Tante* Adri?"

She sighed and Ko preened, at the same time winking at me. *Good answer, Linnet! Good answer!*

Beaming back at him, I went on becoming solicitous.

"How is your headache, *Tante* Adri? Can I do something for you? Would you like me to make you a cup of tea?"

"No, thank you."

Tante Adri's tone had reverted back to being short and irritable. Ko chirruped and shook his left wing. I stood quietly for a moment. It seemed rather apparent that *Tante* Adri was finished interrogating my person. But just as I was about to turn and walk back out, she began to speak again.

"Will you be going back to *Mevrouw* Smit today?"

217

"No, *Tante* Adri. But I will be going there again tomorrow."

"Maybe, Linnet, you could peel some potatoes for supper?"

"Yes, *Tante* Adri."

"Good girl. And are you sure nothing else happened in your schooling today that you want to tell me about?"

"No, I don't think so, *Tante* Adri."

"Well, see you later then, Child."

After having said this, she pressed her head into the pillow and closed her eyes. For a moment, I contemplated her left hand, the hand that had been punished by her grade three teacher. Ko tucked his head into his neck. He was perched on one foot and had the other tucked into its belly. *I'm going to have a little sleep, Linnet. Have fun peeling potatoes.*

I went downstairs again, this time stepping on the creaking board with gusto. I did not have to worry about being heard.

The potatoes were in the back shed, and I carried a cast-iron pan outside. The double doors of the shed were easy to open, and the potatoes stood in the corner, tied up in a burlap bag. Placing a number of them into the pan, I carted the rather heavy load back into the house. Freddy had told me that his grandmother used to clean potatoes by immersing them into a pail of water. Then she had put a broom into the pail and had swished the potatoes about and about. The swishing, Freddy had informed me, made the peels come off very easily. It might be fun to try this theory out, but the pail that I used to clean the kitchen and the bakery floor was not altogether clean. So maybe today was not a good day to put the pail–broom method into practice.

As I set the full pan on the kitchen counter, I heard the bakery doorbell tinkle. As always, I relished the sound. It was so cheerful, so very friendly. But then a harsh voice cut in through the little chime.

"*Wie geht es dir?*"

It was German and very likely the words belonged to a German soldier. After all, no other people in town spoke German. With my heart beginning to thump faster and louder, I stole towards the open doorway. *Pake* had answered the soldier, but I couldn't make out exactly what he had said. Another voice, not the first voice, spoke. So there must be two soldiers.

"*Wo ist der Junge?*"

I didn't quite understand the gist of what the soldier was asking but I did know that the word *Junge* meant "boy."

"He's not here," *Pake* answered briefly.

Who was not here? Whom was *Pake* talking about? Was he talking about Otto? But he had told me that the soldiers were coming to search Oma's house, not the bakery, not our house. He had told me to take Otto here because it would be a safe place for him to hide.

"*Wir suchen Ihr Haus.*"

These words were a mystery to me. But they did not remain a mystery for long, for as I shrank back into the kitchen, boot steps thudded my way. I folded my hands behind my back. Could you pray with your hands folded behind your back?

A moment later the two soldiers, *Pake* flanking their rear, appeared in the doorway of the kitchen.

"Linnet," *Pake's* voice addressed me, "these two gentlemen want to search the house. Will you kindly show them the kitchen?"

I moved aside clumsily, partly tripping over the braided rug by the door. There was not much to show. The soldiers could easily see for themselves that there was only the table, the stove, the window, a closet, the *kachel*, the wood-burning stove, the pan with the potatoes on the counter, and the cupboards above the counter. *Just remember that someone who wants information for the purpose of evil, that person has no right to the truth.* Oma Sanne's words poured over me and I felt as if she was right by my side.

"*Versteckst du jemanden?*"

With no idea what they were asking, I simply stared at them. Their uniforms were not as clean and trim as Jürgen's had been, and their faces were hard and unsympathetic. Maybe these were some of the Germans who did not know God.

"They are asking you if you are hiding someone, Linnet."

Pake's voice was dry as always, and his blue eyes penetrated mine. I shook my head at the soldiers, trying to indicate that I was not hiding anyone in this kitchen. Inside I was so very glad that Otto was not here, that he had gone away with Karel and that my bedroom upstairs had no one hiding in it. The younger soldier opened the closet, rummaged about, and then opened all the drawers below the counter. As if, I thought, someone could hide in a drawer.

"*Ist das Ihre Enkelin?*"

Pake inclined his head to the question.

"*Wo ist deine Frau?*"

Pake pointed towards the stairs. The two soldiers looked at one another. They both shrugged their shoulders, but the younger one disappeared back into the bakery, reappearing a minute later with a few cookies. He began eating one, smacking his lips and grinning at me in a silly manner. It was not in me to grin back so I looked down at the floor. The older one then walked out the back door into the yard, checking out the shed. It was a good thing that Otto had not had to make use of it.

"Wir gehen nach oben."

I wasn't sure what that meant, but after these words, both soldiers turned, left the kitchen, and traipsed through the little hallway towards the stairs. Noiselessly, I stood at the foot and watched the two men clatter up ahead of *Pake*. I wondered what *Tante* Adri would be thinking as she lay in her bed listening to this racket. Was she scared? What would she say to these soldiers? After all, she had asked them to come over. Not here though. She had told them to go next door to Oma Sanne's house. She had informed them that there was a Jewish boy hiding there. Would they go next door after their visit here?

I could hear doors slam, and then after some five minutes of fearful splintering and fracturing noises, *Tante* Adri's terrified voice became audible.

"Leave me alone, you brutes! Leave me alone! Albert!"

There was a loud pop sound, followed by a violent crash. My heart thumped, and I wished that I were somewhere else, somewhere safe, somewhere in my cottage in the dunes. My hands, still folded behind my back, began to pray. *God, please help Tante Adri. Don't let the soldiers hurt her or Pake.*

A few moments later, the two green uniforms stomped down again. They didn't bother to recheck the kitchen, where I was hiding under the table behind its long-hanging tablecloth. They strode past its doorway, tramped on into the shop, and on their way out to the street, knocked down various articles. I could hear glass breaking and tins falling down onto the floor. Crawling out from under the table, I began to cry.

"Linnet."

It was *Pake*. His face was very pale and his right hand, as it held onto the kitchen door handle, showed white at the knuckles.

"Yes, *Pake*." Sobbing the answer, it was all I could do not to scream. I felt taut and ready to snap.

"Linnet, could you make *Tante* Adri a cup of tea? She is quite upset, and I must check the bakery."

"Yes, *Pake*."

I wailed out the answer as he turned abruptly and proceeded on to the bakery rather woodenly, as if he had no joints. My own hands trembled as they rummaged through the cupboard for a cup and a saucer. It was no use. I had to finish my cry first. I walked back to the table and sat down on one of the chairs. No one from the street could see me. And what would they see anyway – just a little girl with her head down on the table.

"Oh, Freddy," I whispered, "I do wish that you were here. But I am a brave soldier, just like you said. I am, Freddy."

I could hear *Pake* picking up broken glass and emptying it into something. There was a distrust in me about the way that things had happened. It was all going much too fast, and I could not attach any rhyme or reason to anything that had occurred today. Who was telling the truth? Who was lying?

Perhaps I should go up and check on *Tante* Adri first, before making tea. Even if she were a big fibber and not a good lady, it could be that those soldiers had hurt her. I sat up, wiped my face on the tablecloth, and then stood up to find the dish towel hanging on the rack by the counter. I blew my nose into it and thought about what Thea would say if she would ever catch me doing such a thing. But Thea wasn't here, and that fact brought added tears to my eyes. I had to blow my nose into the towel once more.

This time up, I bypassed the eighth step, taking a large double-step to avoid it. I could hear Ko clamoring loudly, even before I got to the top of the stairs. It was not his usual talking or whistling or chitter-chatter. He sounded unhappy and upset. I stopped and listened carefully. The little bird was actually screaming. Something was wrong, something was dreadfully wrong, or he would not be making that noise.

Slowly advancing to the bedroom door, I opened it for the second time that afternoon. The first thing I saw was that Ko's cage was not hanging from the ceiling hook any longer. Lying on its side next to the bed, it held an anxious parakeet who was sitting upright, wings raised and head lowered. He looked in the direction of the door as I came in.

"It's all right, Ko," I whispered, but knew that things were not all right, that things were profoundly wrong. In the first place, *Tante* Adri was lying on the bed all curled up, her knees pulled up to her chest, her eyes wide open. She seemed to be gazing out into space, gazing without seeing anything.

"*Tante* Adri?" I mouthed as I advanced, "*Tante* Adri are you all right?"

She didn't answer. She didn't even blink. Down on the ground, Ko blinked. He blinked rapidly, and then squawked loudly. *Something bad has happened, Linnet. Something bad has happened.*

"I know, Ko," I said, and my voice quivered.

Ko's metal chain had been broken off; I could see that at a glance. Part of the chain dangled from the ceiling, and part of it had fallen into the cage itself. Reaching the bed, I bent over and touched *Tante* Adri's hand. Gently I touched it. Her fingers and palm were quite cold. I remembered coming in to Thea when she was in bed, when she was unhappy and crying. It seemed like a very long time ago.

"*Tante* Adri?" I said, and repeated, "Tante Adri?"

She opened her eyes and appeared to see me. "Linnet," she said and she enunciated quite distinctly.

"Yes, *Tante* Adri, I'm here."

"They shot at the cage. It fell onto the ground, and poor Ko fell with it!"

Her eyes filled with tears, and I felt very badly for her. "I think that Ko is not hurt, *Tante* Adri. He's quite lively actually," I reassured her. "He's a little angry, and that why he's squawking so loudly."

"I thought they were going to shoot me, Linnet."

The sentence came out quite pitifully. I remembered seeing brown gun holsters hanging from the belts of the soldiers. Freddy had a belt. But no guns had ever hung from his belt. His belt had just held his pants up.

"They were not very nice, Tante Adri. But they are gone now, and you don't have to worry anymore."

"But will they come back, Linnet? And will they shoot me if they come back?"

Tante Adri's eyes became a trifle glazed, and she suddenly grasped my hand, the hand with which I was stroking her arm. She gripped so hard that I almost cried out in pain.

"Linnet!! Where did that Jewish boy go? He was supposed to come with you. He was supposed to be here in this house."

My mind fogged up some at this point. *Pake* must have told *Tante* Adri about hiding Otto here, and the two of them must have schemed together to hand him over to the German police. If that were true, then they would hand Thea over too, should she come here. I gave all my attention to *Tante* Adri's face and, strangely enough, felt sorry for the sick fanaticism displayed on it.

"You don't even know this boy," I countered. "Why would you want him arrested?"

"Because," she answered, "because all Jewish people are bad."

"Did the snake, the Father of Lies, tell you that?"

I don't know why I said that. It just came out. *Tante* Adri's puffy eyes rounded out in surprise. She twisted my hand in a hurtful way so that I tried to jerk it away.

"You are a rude child and a strange one," she wheezed out, "and I should never have let *Pake* talk me into having you come here. Freddy has never come back to see us, so why on earth we should have agreed to help him take care of his child, I don't know."

Ko had settled down somewhat. He had stopped screeching, and the room was quiet now. I could hear footsteps coming up the stairs. *Tante* Adri loosened her grip on my hand, and I pulled it away, taking a step backwards as I did so. The door behind me opened, and Oma Sanne's voice simultaneously bolstered my courage and my desire to weep.

"*Mevrouw* Smit?" *Tante* Adri's angry voice had camouflaged into friendliness.

'Yes, please forgive me for breaking into your privacy here," Oma spoke softly, "but I could hear the commotion in the bakery and saw the soldiers leave. I just wanted to make sure that you were all right, Adri. And also," and here she smiled at me, "I wanted to make sure that the child was safe."

"Oh, Oma," I wailed, and couldn't help myself. "It was awful. The soldiers were mean and rude, and they shot down Ko's cage. Just look."

"Yes, I can see that they did." As she spoke, she put the Bible, which she was carrying in her hands, down on the night table, and wrapped her arms about me. It felt so good to have someone care.

At this juncture, *Tante* Adri sat up. She swung her feet over the edge of the bed, and regarded both of us with a mixture of jealousy and disgust. But her expression unexpectedly changed to one of fear. Grasping her chest with both of her fleshy hands, she fell sideways onto the bed. Oma let go of me and was by her side in an instant.

"Pressure" *Tante* Adri whispered, "and pain."

"Lie back," Oma ordered. "Just lie back and relax."

"Everything hurts."

I could see from where I was peeking around Oma's back that *Tante* Adri had broken out into a colossal sweat. Big drops beaded on her forehead.

"I think it's your heart, Adri," Oma said, even as she lifted *Tante* Adri's feet back onto the bed. "I want you to lie very quietly. Linnet will go downstairs and tell Albert to go for a doctor."

"Don't go away," *Tante* Adri moaned. "Please don't go, Sanne. I don't want to die alone."

"You know what we'll do while Linnet goes down, Adri? We'll pray together, you and I." Oma Sanne turned her head and raised her eyebrows at me even as she spoke, indicating that I should do what she had just said. I nodded and stiffly walked over to the door.

As I fearfully rushed down the stairs a moment later, I could hear Ko begin complaining loudly.

"*Pake?*" Pake was on his knees, scrubbing the bakery floor with vigor. The pail I used each morning for cleaning stood by his side, brimful with suds. He didn't respond to my call.

"*Pake!*"

Walking over to his side, I touched his shoulder. He looked up, but even as *Tante* Adri's eyes had been unseeing when I had come into the bedroom, so his were also strangely vacant, and I knew that he didn't really see me.

"Pake!" I said for the third time. "*Tante* Adri is sick, and Oma Sanne said you ought to go for a doctor."

"A doctor? I can't go for a doctor. Can't you see that I'm busy and that it's dark outside?"

It was dark outside. I knew that for a fact, even though I couldn't see out the window. The black blinds were always drawn at dusk.

"But, *Pake*," I insisted, "*Tante* Adri is very sick. Oma Sanne thinks it's her heart. Oma Sanne said a doctor should come."

"I can't go for a doctor," he repeated. "It's dark outside. They would arrest me."

"If you tell me where the doctor lives," I offered, "I'll go to his house, *Pake*. Then you won't have to go."

"No," he stubbornly repeated, his eyes on the sudsy water running down the cracks of the floor. "I won't tell you where he lives. Go to your room, Linnet."

The shop bell tinkled, and we both turned. *Pake*, with fear in his eyes, scrambled to his feet, and I stumbled uncertainly as he haphazardly blundered against me.

"Hello, Linnet. Good evening, Mr. Veerman."

It was Karel, and for the second time that day, my joy knew no bounds. "Karel," I sang out again and almost tripped over *Pake's* foot as I sought to pass him.

"Yes, it's me," he grinned as he enveloped me in a bear hug and then held me back so that he could study my face.

"And is my Poppet all right?"

"Yes, I am fine," I answered, although my voice trembled. "How come you're here, Karel?"

"Well, I thought I'd look in on my little friend, Linnet, don't you know? And I also heard that the Germans have been inordinately involved in raiding the bakery today."

"Yes, they were here, Karel. And they broke things in the shop, and they scared me. They were not nice. And upstairs . . . ."

I stopped. Was I talking too much? *Pake* did not appear to be listening. In any case, he was not saying a word, but had dropped back down to his knees and was once more scouring the floor. So I went on.

"They were in *Tante* Adri's bedroom, Karel. And they shot down the birdcage, and *Tante* Adri is sick, and Oma Sanne says she should have a doctor."

"Well, then we'll have to try and get one, won't we."

"Do you know where to find a doctor, Karel?

"Actually, I do. So off I go and, don't you worry, Poppet, I will be back sooner or later."

He let go of my shoulders, and walking backwards, made for the door. Saluting me, he turned and slipped into the dark. *Pake* had paid no attention whatsoever.

"I'll go back upstairs now, *Pake*. Unless you want me to help you clean up."

He did look up now. "No, you go on up, Linnet."

But I didn't. Although I did walk through the small hallway and climb up the stairs, I did not reach the top. Instead, I sat down on the eleventh step and let my feet dangling lightly above the creak. My mind was befuddled and woozy, and some stability came to me in sitting down. *Pake* couldn't see me from where he was in the bakery. Oma and *Tante* Adri couldn't see me either.

Questions lay scattered helter-skelter on every step of the stairs. Where had Karel come from? Had he brought Otto away to some safe place where he would not be seen, where he would not be arrested by the police? Was *Tante* Adri going to be all right? She sure had gripped my arm tightly.

I looked at the skin under the dim hall light shining behind my back. Even in the dull glow available on the stairs, I could see that my wrist was red and tender. Was *Tante* Adri crazy, crazy out of her mind, and to be pitied? Would she have hurt me more if Oma Sanne had not come in? I had no desire to go back to her bedroom, to be nice to her, even if I did wonder how Ko was.

Slowly, I got up and made my way through the hallway to the second stairs. Up the second flight I plodded, step by step, all the while wishing that I was home in the cottage; that I was walking up to my little nook behind the curtains; that soon Thea would come up the stairs as well to tuck me in. *Goodnight, Linnet. I love you.*

It was quite dark in the attic, and through the dimness of the garret my hand reached for the chain that activated the grungy light bulb hanging from the wooden ceiling. Finding it, I pulled. A soft click initiated its harsh glare – a glare which flooded the attic room. German planes might see it, and then we might be bombed. Or a policeman looking up at the stars could potentially notice it from the street, and then he might come traipsing into the bakery.

As these thoughts jumbled through my mind, I quickly ascertained where the bed stood, and was about to pull the chain downward aiming to race for the cot immediately afterwards. But although my feet were ready to travel, I stopped dead in my tracks. For on the floor between myself and the bed was a mousetrap – and an inert, grey little body was contorted in it, beady eyes wide open. It was Freda. Next to her snout lay a piece of hard, yellow cheese.

I switched off the light, yanking the chain so hard that it hurtled up into the air after I let go. *Tante* Adri was mean. It was not as though the mouse had hurt her some time in the past; and it was not as if she believed the mouse to be Jewish. No, she was just plain mean. Maybe *Tante* Adri herself would die before the doctor came to the house. Would I be glad about that?

Sitting down on the edge of the cot in front of the mousetrap, I stared out into the dark. Oma Sanne was still here. Maybe I could go home with her tonight and sleep on her couch. Maybe I should go downstairs and ask her if I might please come to her house.

14

Slowly, step by step, I dawdled my way down the stairs. Transfixed in front of *Tante* Adri's bedroom, I stood for a long while in the hallway. Oma Sanne's voice reached through clearly, whereas *Tante* Adri's words were soft and almost inaudible. Very much wanting to hear what Oma had to say without having to look at *Tante* Adri's face, I eventually sat down, my back against the door, my head leaning sideways against its framework. Periodically *Tante* Adri mumbled incoherently. Her confused words slipped out from under the door, dying on the hall carpet.

"It doesn't matter what we have done, Adri," Oma's voice was unfaltering and sure, "Jesus Christ came to save sinners – sinners like you and me. All we have to do is tell Him that we are sorry for our sins; that we believe in Him; and He will give us eternal life. It could be, Adri, that you will come face to face with Him pretty soon – that you will see Him."

There was an interruption by *Tante* Adri and I could not catch the reply. But Oma's voice passed through the wall without difficulty.

"We are none of us good enough, Adri. We have all of us done things we are sorry for."

For a few moments there was quiet, except that Ko made a few short, sharp sounds, as if he were impatient.

"Don't be afraid, Adri. Remember this saying: 'Perfect love casts out all fear'? It'll be Christmas next month," Oma went on reassuringly. "Don't you remember the Christmas story, Adri?"

I strained against the door, lifting my head slightly. I did not know the Christmas story, but I loved stories. Was Oma going to tell it?

"I have my Bible with me, Adri. Since we've not had supper, let's eat the words God gives us so that we can have full hearts."

Eat words? Like pancakes? Or bread? I was hungry too – hungry for comfort and company.

Even though I was in the hallway, I could clearly picture Oma get up from her chair to reach for the Bible on the night table. Ko would be watching her. He was very quiet right now, probably tuckered out from falling down with his cage. I could visualize Oma sitting back down on the upholstered rattan chair which stood in the left corner next to the bed, the Bible heavy on her lap. I could see her flipping through the pages of her Bible, her blue-veined hands adjusting the spectacles on her nose.

"Please."

Tante Adri's voice was intelligible now, but it was abnormal. It sounded like a mewing, a mewing like Belle the cat made when she wanted to go outside. Oma began to read. Oma had often brought me *koek* from her kitchen and had served me tea. She had made sure that my stomach was filled. Was she filling my heart now too, just like *Tante* Adri's heart?

In those days Caesar Augustus issued a decree that a census should be taken of the entire Roman world. (This was the first census that took place while Quirinius was governor of Syria.) And everyone went to their own town to register. So Joseph also went up from the town of Nazareth in Galilee to Judea, to Bethlehem the town of David, because he belonged to the house and line of David. He went there to register with Mary, who was pledged to be married to him and was expecting a child. While they were there, the time came for the baby to be born, and she gave birth to her firstborn, a son. She wrapped him in cloths and placed him in a manger, because there was no guest room available for them.

I wondered if that baby was the baby Jesus. I distinctly remembered that Oma had told me that Jesus' mother was named Mary. Mary was a lovely name. I didn't know anyone named Mary. There had been Marieke with the red hair. But Marieke was not the same as Mary. I yawned and shivered at the same time, stretching out my arms. My head was sore and my arms and legs ached as well. Closing my eyes, I leaned back into the reading.

I bring you good news that will cause great joy for all the people. Today in the town of David a Savior has been born to you; He is the Messiah, the Lord. This will be a sign to you: You will find a baby wrapped in cloths and lying in a manger.

What was a manger? I didn't know that word. The baby was wrapped in cloths. I had been wrapped in a white blanket when I was in the wooden box. Thea had told me this, and I had worn a bonnet with stars on it. God made the stars on the fourth day. That's what it said in the Bible. He had made the sun and the moon on that day too. And then the next day He had made the birds and the fish. And then, well then, I suppose I fell asleep for a minute, because my head dropped downwards. And that woke me up again.

On the eighth day, when it was time to circumcise the child, he was named Jesus, the name the angel had given him before he was conceived.

I smiled to myself. Yes, I had been right. The baby that was born in the manger and wrapped in cloths was Jesus.

"Do you remember, Adri," Oma's voice went on inside the bedroom. "Do you remember what the name 'Jesus' means?"

Tante Adri must have nodded or something, because I couldn't hear her response at all. Or maybe she had forgotten what "Jesus" meant, or maybe she just didn't know. I surely didn't know.

"'Jesus' means," Oma went on, "'Savior.' That is to say, He will save His people from their sins."

Tante Adri moaned. I could hear her clearly through the door, and the sound made my spine tingle. It was such a sad sound, such a hopeless sound, and such a very lonely sound. In spite of what had happened, I suddenly found myself feeling sorry for her.

"Don't fret, Adri," Oma said, her voice filled with compassion, and I could hear her moving about in the room. "Let me give you a drink of water. I surely expected the doctor by now, but we will be fine, you and I, and I will stay with you."

I was almost jealous of the loving tone that Oma poured out on *Tante* Adri. It was like a blanket, soft and warm. For a few minutes, there was no noise other than a few tranquil chirrups from Ko. *Tante* Adri must have been drinking. But as I relaxed against the door, her voice unexpectedly and urgently broke through the paneled wood again.

"I'm not ready, Sanne! I'm not ready! I've got . . . I've got some things to say and do before . . . I've got to pay, you see . . . ."

"You know, Adri," Oma's words soothed, "it really doesn't matter, Girl. It's all been paid for. If you believe in the Lord Jesus Christ, He has paid for your sins."

There was quiet for a long moment. I studied my brown, scuffed shoes. What did *Tante* Adri want to say, and to whom did she want to say it? Whom did she want to pay? Inarticulate and muddled words traveled under the door into the hallway, words that I could not quite make out.

"Don't take on so," Oma responded to whatever it was that *Tante* Adri had tried to say. "Don't be so tormented. A little while ago, we asked the Lord Jesus to forgive your sins. Remember? Let me tell you one more time. When you are sorry for your sins, the Lord Jesus gives you salvation. He gives it to you for nothing.

Tante Adri coughed raucously and called out a ragged, "Free?!"

"Yes, free, Adri," Oma soothed, "Jesus has prepared a room for you – a beautiful room. After you die and stand before God, He will say, 'Adri, your sins have been paid for. Here is your room! It is free! It won't cost you anything! It was paid for by the Lord Jesus. You need not worry about paying the price.'"

Tante Adri didn't reply, but I could hear her weeping hoarsely. Something for nothing. The words danced around in my brain. Something paid for by someone else. Was that such a strange thing? Was it something to cry about?

I was transported back to the island. It was a Thursday morning, and it was the very first time that I had been sent on my own to the store by Thea. She had given me a piece of paper with a list of items written on it which I was to pick up.

"Now where is the list, Linnet?"

"In my pocket."

"Can you take it out and read it to me?"

Carefully I extracted the blue-lined paper, smoothed it out on my frock, and began to read the items on it.

"Two loaves of white bread, a package of *biscuit,* (biscuits), and twelve raisin buns."

"Very good," Thea praised. "Now don't lose the list, and you'll be fine. Hang on to your green bag carefully. And don't stop to talk to the seagulls."

"Aw, Thea," I responded, rather miffed that she would think I would lose either the bag or the list.

"All right, Little Thing, march along then."

I turned and began my trek past the pump, out the gate, and onto the sand lane. Very aware of Thea's eyes on my back, I almost didn't wave. But then, thinking of how pleased she would be to get a wave, I veered around and, trotting backwards, waved the green bag like a flag. She grinned and waved back.

"Goodbye, Linnet!"

"Goodbye, Thea!"

It was a glorious day for walking. The dunes were oozing warmth and peacefulness, the sky was blue, and the air was fresh. I arrived at the village in no time at all. Nothing had distracted me and, self–satisfied, I swung my green bag with abandon. Every now and then, I would put my hand into my pocket and touch the list that Thea had written out for me with such great care. I had it memorized anyway – two loaves of white bread, *beschuit*, rusks, and twelve raisin buns. Thea would be so proud of me when I came home with these things, and so would Freddy.

The bakery shop was closer now, and I could see from a distance that I would not be the only one visiting the shop that morning. Several people clustering at the entrance disappeared inside. I had never been in the bakery without Thea or Freddy before this. Unconsciously, my back straightened and my fingers covertly crept into my pocket to connect with the list again, just in case my memory happened to fail me. Then I moved along briskly. Imagine if those other people had designs on buying all the raisin buns!

Before I arrived at the shop, the bell attached to the door of the bakery clanged once more. This time, a boy entered, a boy quite a bit older than myself. Before the ringing metal sound had died away I came to the entrance. At this juncture, I began to miss Thea just a bit. To pick up groceries had sounded easy in the cottage kitchen, but now with the shop rather full of strangers, conditions seemed just a bit more daunting and difficult. I took a deep breath, pulled the door open, and walked in. That is to say, I tripped in, for the mat at the doorway caught the toe of my shoe and I stumbled forward.

Dropping the green bag, I went flying, scraping my knee in the process. The boy laughed, and I swallowed away ready tears threatening to escape my eyes. Not only did the boy begin to laugh, he also began to sing:

"Rock–a–bye, baby, on the bakery floor."

The other customers in the store looked over their shoulders and smiled, and I flushed a deep red as I picked myself up. Retrieving up my bag, I footed it towards the corner, ignoring everyone and pretending to be totally immersed in all the wonderful pastries displayed in and around the bakery counter. After paying, the first customers left carrying out some pastry. The second customers, a man and a woman, bought three loaves of bread. As the man took out his wallet to pay, it suddenly struck me with horrible clarity that I carried no wallet and that I did not possess even a single penny. It took a full minute for this to sink in. Consequently, I was not listening when the boy addressed me.

"Hey, Little Girl," he said. "You can go ahead of me if you like. I'm not in a hurry."

I immediately shook my head,

"No, thank you."

He shrugged and walked over to the counter. Fingering the shopping list which was rapidly becoming crinkled with the overuse of my sweaty hands, I contemplated walking out of the store. Had Thea just forgotten to give me some money? Out of the corner of my eye, I could see that the boy was counting out several coins into his right hand. Nonchalantly, I tried to regress to the door. It was too late. The lady behind the counter was finished with the boy and she brightly called out to me.

"Hello, Linnet. Have you come for some bread?"

I nodded, unable to speak.

"Do you have a list with you," she asked kindly. "If you give it to me, I'll read it and make sure you get everything on it."

I reached into my pocket and gave her the crumpled, damp paper. With the boy gone, I was now the only customer in the store.

"Well," the lady said, and her name was Anna, for I had heard Thea call her that. "How about a cookie while you are waiting."

"No, thank you."

I did manage those words, thinking that if I was to get into trouble for not having money, having a cookie would only make matters worse for me.

"No, to a cookie? Linnet, are you feeling all right?"

I nodded.

"Well, all right then. Let's see now," Anna spoke as she studied the list carefully. "I think I can manage to fill your bag. How about handing it up to me."

With a heavy heart, I lifted the green bag up to her outstretched arm.

"Good girl," Anna cheerfully sang out. "And isn't it a beautiful day today? And how is Freddy?"

"Fine."

"Well, you're not very talkative today, are you?"

With greater and greater trepidation, I watched her fill my green bag with the loaves, with *beschuit*, and with raisin buns."

The closer the green bag came to being full, the harder my heart began to thump. Walking out from behind the counter, Anna smilingly handed me the carryall.

"Hope it's not too heavy for you," she remarked. "And you know what? You might not feel like a treat now, but suppose you take something for on the road later?

Before I knew what had happened, she had inserted a large chunk of *speculaas* between the thumb and fingers of my left hand.

"I don't have any money. I can't pay," I stuttered out at this point, "so you might want to take everything out of the bag again."

"Can't pay?" she repeated, studying my face with a mixture of curiosity and misapprehension. "But you silly goose, you don't have to pay. It's free. Freddy paid for you yesterday when he passed through town."

"Linnet! Linnet!"

Someone was shaking me, and opening my eyes in bewilderment, I did not quite know where I was.

"Linnet, Poppet, please get up so that the good doctor can go into the bedroom." Karel was standing over me in the hallway. A tall, dark-haired man stood behind him, a man carrying a black, leather case.

I scrambled to my feet, and Karel took my hand even as he opened the door to *Tante* Adri's bedroom. Oma Sanne was sitting in the rattan chair in the corner of the bedroom. She looked tired, and no wonder, she had been nursing *Tante* Adri for a long, long time.

"How is the patient?" the doctor inquired, striding over to the bed. "I'm sorry I couldn't come sooner, but I was delivering a baby and unable to leave. Besides that, the restrictions on traveling after curfew made getting here rather slow and tiresome, not to speak of dangerous."

Karel and I followed the doctor into the room even as he spoke. Oma did not answer the doctor's question, but simply indicated by a turn of her head that he should take a look for himself. *Tante* Adri had not moved at all when we came in. Her eyes were closed and remained closed. I did not like to look at her, so I switched my gaze to Ko. The bird was standing on one leg, his four toes firmly grasping the wooden perch, his head tucked into his feathers and his eyes closed – closed just like Tante Adri's eyes.

"How long?" the doctor softly asked Oma.

"About fifteen minutes ago," she replied.

Karel pulled my hand and steered me back into the hallway. "Well, Poppet," he remarked, "it's been quite a day for you."

I stared up at him, unable to say anything. He regarded me for a long moment, concern and love flowing from his eyes.

"Well, Poppet," he repeated, "we'll wait for Oma downstairs, and perhaps you can stay with her tonight."

"Oh, yes," I breathed, feeling flushed and rather unsteady. "You see, Freda is dead and lying in front of my cot upstairs, and I don't want to go back there."

"Freda?" he answered in a perplexed way, furrows beginning to groove on his forehead. "And who is Freda, Linnet?"

"My mouse," I replied, and he smiled at that, at the same time lifting me up and carrying me in his arms like a little child.

At any other time, I might have protested. After all, I was going to be six, next month. At this moment, however, I was glad of the security of his body and the shelter of his being. And I felt so very tired, so extremely weary that I could hardly think.

"Do you have another letter for me, Karel," I whispered into his ear.

"Another letter? Two in one day? You should be so fortunate."

"If I write a letter to Freddy and Thea, will you take it to them?"

"That I will, Poppet," he answered as we clopped down the stairs. "That I will. But for now, I have to speak with your *Pake*. "

15

There was a haziness throughout the hours and days that followed. I only knew that my head ached badly and my muscles were unwilling to cooperate. Sometimes, I was aware that someone was giving me spoonfuls of broth or a drink, and at other times, I was vaguely conscious of the fact that there was a person sitting by my bedside. Only my bed was not in the attic, because the ceiling no longer consisted of wooden beams. I tried very hard to figure this out, to ascertain where I was, but could not come to any conclusion. Every time I tried to sit up, dizziness and blackness would overpower me, and I would lie back down, my eyes shutting of their own accord.

When at length I came to my senses to the point of focusing directly, I saw that Karel was sleeping in a chair next to my bed and that Ko's birdcage was dangling from the ceiling. I blinked and willed my mind to concentrate.

"Hello, Ko," I whispered softly, but not so soft that it didn't waken Karel.

"Well, and if it isn't my poppet waking up," he boomed out, and then, adding much softer, "I'm so glad to see you, and weren't we that worried that . . . . Well, never mind what we were worried about, but your eyes were so . . . ."

I smiled and yawned broadly.

"Yes," Karel laughed, "yawn, you Sleeping Beauty, for it is a hundred years that you have been asleep. And I'm your Prince Charming, Poppet."

"Where am I?"

"Where are you? Why you're at Oma Sanne's house, Poppet, and she's been nursing you devotedly for a few days now."

"Oma Sanne's?"

"Yes, and she's having a well-deserved nap, you've so tuckered her out."

"I'm sorry."

"Oh, Poppet, old Karel is only kidding. She is only too happy to have you here. She loves you."

"Freddy and Thea?"

"Why, they're fine."

"And *Pake*?"

"*Pake*? Well, he's a bit confused, Linnet. He's mostly down at the bakery, cleaning, and baking, and selling bread. Only he doesn't talk much."

"*Tante* Adri?"

"Well, she's buried, Poppet. Buried in the graveyard behind the church up the hill. I expect that when you're all better, you might want to go and have a look-see but that's still a long way away."

I tried to sit up, but could not manage it. All this time, Ko had been perched on his wooden rung but had not chirped at all. "Did you bring Ko over?"

"I did, and fixed the cage, and hung it from the ceiling. But the bird is rather speechless, Poppet. His little feet were clenched to his perch when I moved him, and although his claws have now relaxed, he's not sung a note since all this business has happened."

"Hello, Ko," I whispered again, but the bird neither raised his head nor looked at me, and I really wanted to go over and stroke his green feathers.

"Do you know God, Karel, and His Son Jesus?"

"Now, why do you ask me that, Poppet?"

Karel shifted in his chair, and I closed my eyes. I slightly remembered a number of things, and they had to do with God.

"Because God is free, Karel. He lets you into heaven if you believe in Him. It's true, because I heard Oma Sanne say so."

Karel sighed but didn't say a word.

"Karel?"

"Yes, Poppet."

"Can you write a letter to Freddy and Thea for me?"

"Now, that I can do. Let's see, I think Oma Sanne has some paper in a desk here and yes . . . . "

As Karel spoke he reached back and began to rummage through an oak bureau behind him, extracting a writing pad and a pencil. "If you write with your mouth," he joked, "I will jot it down on the paper."

I smiled and wiggled my toes under the blanket. Even that took a lot of effort.

"Did I almost die?" I asked, eyes on Karel's bulky form as he stretched up his right leg to make some sort of tabletop out of his knee.

"We were worried, Poppet," he replied.

I was quiet a long moment. "Did Freddy and Thea know?"

"Well, I did speak to them once, but did not want to worry them."

My eyes suddenly sprang full of tears. Karel was all solicitousness.

"Hey now, Little Soldier. You've fought your battle bravely. No need to drown that blanket there," he kidded, even as he put the pencil behind his right ear, took a big white hanky out of his pocket, reached over, and gently wiped my eyes, "Now then, what do you want to say to Freddy and Thea?"

He sat down again and took the pencil out from behind his ear. I began, began slowly.

Dear Freddy and Thea:

Karel is writing this letter for me. He will take it to you.

At this point I looked at Karel questioningly and he nodded. "Of course I will, Poppet."

I am lying in bed right now and am very tired. I was a little bit sick, but not as sick as you, Thea. I am staying at Oma Sanne's house now, and when I am downstairs, I can see your bakery from the window, Freddy.

Tante Adri died. She was so scared when the German soldiers came over that, I guess, her heart stopped beating. When I am very scared, my heart beats very fast, almost too fast, and I have a hard time talking. But hers stopped. She truly was sorry for the nasty things she did, and cried before she died. I know, because I heard her talk when I was sitting in the hall.

Please write back because I miss you and I love you.

Your Little Thing, Linnet
P.S. I know about God now and about Jesus.

I stopped dictating and was quite tired again. My eyes would not stay open. In the distance, I could hear Karel softly get up and leave the room. It was so nice and warm under the blankets. The attic had been cold, quite cold. I snuggled and took one last look at Ko before I went back to sleep.

"Goodnight, Ko," and I was sure that he chirped back at me, *Goodnight, Linnet.*

When next I opened my eyes, Karel had gone, but Oma was sitting in his spot. She was knitting, and it looked like a sock was dangling from the needles. Her eyes were closed, but her fingers were moving at a speed that was amazing. The sock was blue. It was my favorite color. Was she knitting socks for me? Her eyes opened suddenly and traveled to my face. Dropping her stitches into her lap, she smiled.

"Linnet, my little girl, how long have you been watching me?"

I smiled back. "For a long time, Oma."

"Karel told me that you had been awake. He was so happy to see you get a bit better. He's been here almost every day since you became sick."

"How long was I sick, Oma?"

"Oh, about four days."

"I wrote a letter to Freddy and Thea, Oma."

"Yes, Karel told me that you did. It was kind of him to write it down for you."

"Is he gone to bring it to them, Oma?"

"I believe so."

"Oma?"

"Yes, Linnet."

"Oma, did you go to the funeral for Tante Adri?"

"Yes, I did, although I did not want to leave you alone too long. Karel stayed with you at that time."

"Did *Pake* go to the funeral too?"

"Yes, he did."

"Is he all right?"

"Well, I'm not quite sure he understands everything that has happened. He's still getting up early each morning at four, and he bakes his bread and his cookies. One of the neighbor boys has offered to help him, and I do believe that is going all right, but it's too early to tell."

"Will I have to go back to the attic when I'm better, Oma?"

"No, Linnet. You can stay here."

I breathed a sigh of relief. "Did *Tante* Adri go to the room in heaven, Oma? The room you were telling her about? The one that is free?"

"I think she did, Linnet."

I sighed.

"Is it still war, Oma?"

"Yes, it is."

"Are you making me some socks, Oma?"

"You know, Little Girl," she answered, "you are asking entirely too many questions."

When Thea answered like that about something she was making, I always knew that what she was making was for me. So I smiled.

"Thank you, Oma."

"I think I will go down and warm up some soup for our dinner. How about that, Linnet?"

I smiled and Oma came over, fluffed the pillow under my head, and gave me a kiss. "Well, just have another snooze, Little Girl. After all, you've been working so hard."

I grinned and turned on my side so that I could watch Ko in his cage.

That evening, Oma, sitting by my bedside, told me more about Jesus.

"Have you ever seen a bridge, Linnet?"

"Not on the island, Oma. But I know what a bridge is, and if there was one from the island to the mainland, then we wouldn't have had to cross over in the boat."

Oma smiled. "Yes, that's true. So you know that a bridge brings a person from one point to another. A bridge lets you cross over."

I nodded. "Yes, Oma."

"Well, Jesus is a bridge too, Linnet. He is the bridge between God and you. Like Adam and Eve, you've been thrown out of the garden because of sin. Do you remember the story?"

I did remember. Ko chippered a bit under his wing. I was glad that he was beginning to make sounds again.

"God can't abide our sin, Linnet," Oma went on, unmindful of the tweedling, "but when Jesus carries you in His arms, He covers you Himself. This way God does not see your sins. They are covered by Jesus."

Freddy carried me sometimes. It was when I couldn't walk myself. Karel had carried me too. I didn't quite remember that so well, because I had been sick. Even *Pake* had carried me to bed that first night I had come to the bakery.

"Did *Tante* Adri know about being carried by Jesus, Oma?

"I think so, Linnet."

"What is a manger, Oma?"

"It is a feeding crib, a box from which animals in a barn eat."

"A wooden box?"

"Yes, I suppose it is."

Before she tucked me in for the night, Oma began to teach me a song, a prayer. She said I could sing before I went to sleep each night. I had never done that before.

Weary, lay me down to sleep,
Close my eyes, oh Lord, and keep,
My small being through the night,
Stay with me til morning light.

Evil which I entered in,
Oh, forgive me Lord, my sin,
Though my wrongs me guilty make,
Pardon them for Jesus' sake.

Amen

Christine Farenhorst

"What is pardon, Oma?"
"Pardon means forgiveness, Linnet."

I thought about all these things later, before going to sleep. I considered that I had also been born, or found, at any rate, in a box when I was a baby. A box wasn't quite the same, of course, as a manger, but nevertheless, the small similarity made me feel special. Oma had told me that Jesus called His children, and that those children, after hearing His voice calling them, followed Him. I could understand that. *Baby ducks know their mother when they hatch. This is called imprinting.* That's what Freddy had taught me a long time ago. Freddy was so smart. He had gone on to teach me that when baby ducks or other birds imprinted, they always trailed behind their mother. *They follow their mother, Linnet because they have imprinted on her.*

When had I imprinted on Jesus? When had I first seen Him? I truly did not know. But I knew in my heart that I was following. Had it happened when I met Jürgen ? I could see the dunes and remembered the time that I was looking for periwinkles. And in the remembering, I almost returned to the island, in that I could feel the wind sweep across the strand and the sea, causing the waves to crest up and fall down. And an imperceptible knowledge crept over me that my life was controlled by wind.

I woke up to the sound of something I did not quite recognize. Slowly opening my eyes, I remembered that I was in Oma Sanne's house, and that there were new noises to which I must become accustomed. I turned onto my side to wish Ko a good morning. To my

250

surprise, I noticed something was lying on the floor next to my bed, only it was not a something. It was a person. And that person was making an almost inaudible snorkeling sound.

He or she was covered so totally by a blanket, that I could not make out who it was. The sound made me grin. But who was it? Surely Oma would not be able to sleep on the floor like that. The small size of the form under the blanket told me it was not Karel. Perhaps it was another Otto, someone who needed a home for awhile because the Green Police were looking for him.

But Karel had taken Otto, and Oma would have told me if someone else were coming. But maybe not. I had a great need to make use of the W.C., and carefully I pulled back the covers and put my left leg over the edge of the bed. Ko peeked at me from under his wing. *Hello, Linnet. Are you feeling better?*

The truth was that I was a little wobbly, but I could manage. I put my finger over my lips to warn Ko that he should not make any noise and wake up the stranger. The little snorkeling sound bubbled out, and I grinned. Then I stopped, and my heart began to beat fast and faster. There was only one person in the whole world that I knew made that sound, and she was often teased about it. And that person was Thea. But Thea was in Rotterdam, and she was still ill.

I walked backwards out of the bedroom, went to the bathroom, and returned. Yes, I had not dreamt it. There was a person here. I sat back down on the edge of the bed and studied the form meticulously. There was breathing – up and down, up and down – and every now-and-then, a little snorkel. Freddy used to tease Thea. *My little wife snores.* And she would pretend to be very angry and hit him over the head with a pillow.

I do not. If anyone snores, it's my husband.

Very cautiously, I bent over and lifted up the edge of the coverlet. Very slowly, I lowered my gaze to the head which had been concealed under it. But the hair, the black, curly hair which I had been hoping to see was not there. Instead, nut-brown curls stared up at me. It wasn't Thea.

I burrowed down under the covers of my bed again. Disappointment, dismay, and letdown threatened to overcome me. I felt tears welling up in my throat, and I tried very hard to swallow them. I had been so hopefully sure. That sound, that tiny sound, was exactly the sound that Thea made when she was sleeping. A sob escaped my entire being, and I hid my face under the pillow. I held my breath and pinched my hand. It wouldn't be kind to wake up whoever it was sleeping on the floor.

"Little Thing." A hand touched my shoulder. I felt it through the blanket. But I refused to sit up.

"Little Thing."

I lay very quiet, almost not breathing. The hand moved the blanket and began to stroke the top of my head. It stroked so sweetly that I turned my face upward. But I kept my eyes closed – closed tightly so that I would not see that it was someone else, someone other than my Thea.

"Open your eyes, Linnet." It was Thea's voice.

I opened my eyes and beheld a Thea who had been made over into another person.

"Thea?"

"It's me, Little Thing. It's really me. I know I look a little different with my hair a new color. But I had to change it so that I would look like . . . ."

She stopped. I had flung my arms around her neck and pulled her down for a hug.

"Oh, Thea. I knew you would come back for me. I just knew that you would." And I laughed and cried at the same time, and Ko woke up, loudly squawking and chittering all at the same time.

"Of course, I came back, Little Thing. How could I not? Only I was so sick and couldn't even walk."

"I know, Thea," I said, even as I touched her cheeks and hugged her again and again.

"I got your letter yesterday," she began, "and when I read it, I knew that I had to come as soon as I could. I knew that I had to see you and take care of you again, Little Thing."

"Oh, Thea," I whispered, "I have so much to tell you. I think that my heart is so full of words that they will fall out and knock you over."

****

"The wind blows wherever it pleases. You hear its sound, but you cannot tell where it comes from or where it is going. So it is with everyone born of the Spirit." And a seed planted and destined by God for eternity always sprouts and sends forth its shoots at the correct pace and at the right time.

Glossary of German, Dutch and Frisian Words

Auf wiedersehen - goodbye, till next time

Beschuit - rusk

Boterkoek - buttercake

Das Būch der Būcher - the Book of Books

Der Gūte Gott - the good God

Die Bibel - the Bible

Die Taschen - pockets

Dorp - village

Ein wunderbare Familie - a wonderful family

Gestapo - German police

Grune Polizei - green uniformed police

Heit - Dad, father

Höflich - polite, courteous

In der Tat - indeed

Ist das Ihre Enkelin? - Is that your granddaughter?

Ja - yes

Juffrouw - Miss

Kachel - wood or coal burning stove

Kamerad - comrade

Kansel - pulpit

Kenntnisreich - knowledgeable

Kleines Mädchen - little girl

Koek – cake

Mädchen - young girl

Mem - Mom, mother

Mein kleiner Mädchen - my little girl

Meneer - Mister

Mevrouw - Mrs.

Nachtigal - nightingale

Niemand - no one

Orgel - organ

Pake - grandfather

Portemonnaie - wallet

Schnecke - snails

SD - a Nazi Party intelligence service

Sehr wichtig - very important

Sie heisst Emma - her name is Emma

SS - elite German armed guard

Strandschnecke - periwinkles

Süss - sweet

Tante - aunt

Versteckst du jemanden? - Are you hiding someone?

Vredenhof - Peace Garden

Vuurtoren - fire tower, the light house

Wie gehts? - How are you?

Wie geht es dir? - How are you?

Wir gehen nach oben - We are going upstairs

Wilhelmus - Dutch national anthem

The New Has Come

Words to the Dutch National Anthem:

William of Nassau am I, of German descent;
True to the Fatherland I remain until death.
Prince of Orange am I, free and fearless.
To the King of Spain I have always given honor.

Wir suchen Ihr Haus - We will search your house
Wo ist deine Frau? - Where is your wife?
Wo ist der Junge? - Where is the boy?

Endnote

It was on May 5, 1945, that Holland was liberated. However, the last of the Germans did not leave the island of Schiermonnikoog until June 11, 1945. Because it was surrounded by the sea, it lay isolated from the mainland. At the point of liberation, approximately 120 SD interrogation officers and SS officers who had been stationed in Groningen, as well as some Dutch collaborators, fled to the island. These were cruel men who had imprisoned and brutally tortured and executed Dutch men and women in the infamous Scholtenhuis. Very leery of this group of fanatics, Thomas Wittko, the German commander, moved them to three farms on the east side of the island. Even though Holland had been liberated, Wittko was so nervous as to what this group might do, he did not dare remove the swastika emblem from his cap.

Although Thomas Wittko was interested in capitulating, those of the SD and SS party who had fled to the island for refuge, were not. On May 25, a Dutch man by the name of Herman Kloppenborg, disguised as a Canadian officer and with 2 other Canadian officers, went to the island. The SD and SS group were told that a delegation of Canadians was ready to negotiate. Both sides met, and Herman Kloppenberg, divulging that he had critical information about all the men in question, promised that the entire group would be treated as prisoners of war. They agreed and on May 31, the entire SS and SD group was transferred to the mainland by 2 boats. They were brought to a house of detention in Groningen where they were locked up.

On June 11, 1945, the original German occupiers left the island with Commander Wittko marching in front of his soldiers. At this point the island was finally totally liberated. As Schiermonnikoog was considered enemy property, it was confiscated by the Dutch State on December 17, 1945. Although von Bernstorff tried to regain control of the island, he failed. He later demanded compensation from the German state and in 1983 was given 80,000 Deutsche Mark.

Count Bechtold Eugen von Bernstorff died in 1987 and was buried on the island.

Manufactured by Amazon.ca
Bolton, ON

27919306R00144